THÉODORE DE BANVILLE

MAGIC LANTERN

TRANSLATED AND WITH AN INTRODUCTION BY
BRIAN STABLEFORD

THIS IS A SNUGGLY BOOK

Anthology and Introduction Copyright © 2024
by the Estate of Brian Stableford.
All rights reserved.

ISBN: 978-1-64525-159-0

CONTENTS

INTRODUCTION

La Lanterne magique by Théodore de Banville (1823-1891) was published in book form by G. Charpentier in 1883, but its individual inclusions had previously appeared, in a very different order, between 26 May 1882 and 1 December 1882[1] in the newspaper *Gil Blas*, to which the author had been supplying weekly copy since the end of 1879. In the Charpentier edition the 120 vignettes making up *La Lanterne magique* were followed by an even greater number of *Camées parisiens* [Parisian Cameos], consisting of brief character studies, mostly of real contemporary individuals but including some figures from the past and a few fictitious characters. Many were reprinted from three volumes of *Les Camées parisiens* issued between 1866 and 1873, which had provided a model for the curt style, flippancy and organization into sets of twelve recapitulated in the 1883 volume. The *avant-propos* [preface] of the 1883 book introduces the *Camées* and an appendix first published as a pamphlet, *La Comédie Française racontée par untémoin de ses fautes* (1863) as well as *La Lanterne magique*; I have reproduced that *avant-propos* in full in the preface of the present volume, rather than cut it short so that it only refers to the translated texts, because it helps to provide some useful context.

In 1882 Banville was contracted to supply two weekly columns of approximately 2,000 words to *Gil Blas*, which ap-

---

1 These dates are misrendered in the Charpentier edition, being attributed to 1883 rather than 1882 and the first date being given as 20 May rather than 26 May.

peared on different days—an arrangement similar to those the paper had with two of his younger colleagues, Armand Silvestre (1837-1901) and Jean Richepin (1849-1926); the former had first met Banville in the 1860s,[1] when the two had been associated with a group of poets whom critics subsequently labeled as "Parnassians," after a set of showcase anthologies of their work entitled *Le Parnasse contemporain* (1866-76), edited by Catulle Mendès (1841-1909) and Louis-Xavier Ricard. Mendès also joined the staff of *Gil Blas* while *La Lanterne magique* was being serialized there, initially only supplying one column per week, like most of the paper's other regular columnists. *La Lanterne magique* was serialized in Banville's Friday column, and ran in parallel with two series featured sporadically in his Sunday column, one headlined *Petits Études* [Little Studies] which had been launched in March 1881 and the other headlined *Paris Vécu* [Paris Experienced][2] launched in November 1881.

The *études* were sketches not dissimilar to the *camées*, although considerably longer and more wide-ranging, often taking in groups of people rather than individuals, but *Paris vécu* (also reprinted in volume form by Charpentier as *Petits études: Paris vécu* with *Feuilles volantes* in 1883) was a more coherent serial consisting of a series of letters addressed to "mon Cher Louis," the notional author of which undertakes to explain Parisian society to his correspondent, whose own son, a medical student, has recently relocated to the city; in order to do so, the notional author draws upon his rich past experience of Parisian life. The text is a curious hybrid of fiction and non-fic-

---

1 Richepin also claimed to have first made contact with the Parnassians in the 1860s, but his retrospective accounts of that period in his life, after which he claimed to have been a sniper in the France-Prussian War and then lived as a vagabond, might not be entirely reliable.

2 The range of meaning of the term *vécu* extends a little further than this; it sometimes refers simply to something past, but can also mean something real (as opposed to imaginary) and is also sometimes used to mean something finished.

tion, the commentary including many fictitious anecdotes, such as a series of conversations with one Eugène Dupin, the son of Edgar Poe's Auguste Dupin. Like *La Lanterne magique*, therefore, *Paris vécu* is an unusual literary experiment—highly unusual in the context of a daily newspaper.

When the two Sunday series that ran in parallel with *La Lanterne magique* had begun in 1881 they had run in parallel with another experimental series of short stories, published under the rubric of *Contes fantastiques* in the newspaper but subsequently collected as *Contes féeriques* (1882; tr. as *Magical Tales*). There is a sense in which *La Lanterne magique* is an extension of the *Études*, expanding their scope from real individuals to entirely hypothetical ones, and substituting "snapshots" of imaginary scenes for "pen portraits" of people, but a minority of the inclusions can also be seen as extensions of the *contes fantastiques*, substituting brief "vignettes" for "full length" short stories—"full length," in this context, meaning the fixed length of a newspaper column, then approximately 2,000 words in *Gil Blas*. The columns headlined "La Lanterne Magique" contained between four and six individual items (and in one instance—the column featuring items individually titled for the deadly sins—seven).

Banville's preface in the Charpentier volume likens the vignettes to the items assembled in classic collections of prose vignettes by Alpusius Bertrand and Charles Baudelaire. Bertrand's *Fantaisies à la manière de Rembrandt et Callot par Gaspard de la Nuit* was first published in 1842 and Baudelaire's *Le Spleen de Paris* in 1869 (posthumously, in his *Oeuvres*), but the latter project had begun publication in *La Revue fantaisiste* in 1862 as "Poèmes en prose," and was frequently reprinted as *Petits poèmes en prose*. The latter title lent its label to an entire genre that attempted to carry the endeavor further,[1] but it is

---

1 The history of the genre in question is elaborately detailed in *Poems in Prose: A Showcase Anthology* (Snuggly Books 2024).

unlikely that the author cited that Baudelairean label when offering his proposal to *Gil Blas*, as it might have been more likely to be a deterrent than a selling point in regard to a popular daily newspaper. The label had been featured before in *Gil Blas*, however, in one of Armand Silvestre's columns (17 November 1880), which had grouped four vignettes under the headline *Les Farces de la Lune*, adding the sub-heading *Petits poèmes en prose*. It was not the last time that Silvestre split a column in that fashion, nor was Banville the only colleague of his to imitate the tactic, but it was rare for any of them to use the subtitle "poèmes en prose" and its initial use by Silvestre could easily have been construed as a joke.

Banville had probably had to be ingenious in order to persuade the editors of *Gil Blas* to allow him to carry out his various experiments in literary form and style, including the initial experiment of substituting short fiction for orthodox journalistic commentary in his weekly column, although Silvestre sometimes did the same, and so did some of the paper's other columnists—including Richepin—on occasion. In a broad sense, that experiment had been successful, at least while Banville was producing naturalistic stories rather than fantastic ones, to the extent that such fiction not only became a standard comedic feature in the politically neutral and solidly bourgeois *Gil Blas* but was imitated and further developed by several other daily newspapers, including some that had political agendas and tried to appeal to more proletarian readers.

The stories published in *Gil Blas* were adapted to the mildly satirical environment of the paper, but many of the other newspapers that employed the tactic did not emphasize humor to the same extent, and the fiction they featured was more wide-ranging in its tone and rhetoric. In addition to the primacy of the humorous aspect of his fiction, while working for *Gil Blas* Banville evidently made the assumption—or was instructed by his editors—that his fiction ought to be aimed primarily at female readers; the first series of stories that he published in his weekly column was, in fact, reprinted in volume form as *Contes pour les femmes* [Tales for Wives] (1881) and had clearly been planned with that inclination in mind. The volume was reprinted several times, achieving larger sales than the author's subsequent collections.

Those contextual circumstances introduced a certain tension into Banville's work for *Gil Blas*, because he not only affected to loathe the supposed values of the contemporary *bourgeoisie* and their alleged effect on literary culture, but he also had a rather confused attitude to the fair sex, which he affected to adore on principle, but in a strangely misogynistic, or at least profoundly sexist, manner, the paradoxical aspect of which is starkly obvious in many of the vignettes in the present collection. That perversely ironic aspect of his work is not deleterious to its esthetic appeal—and, indeed, might be regarded as one of its strengths—but it must have made the task of making up short stories and vignettes, week after week, a trifle complicated. Naïve observers might wonder why he did not simply work for more sympathetic employers, but he was a thoroughly professional writer, and he had spent his entire forty-year career making necessary compromises in order to be able to publish work in mildly or ferociously hostile circumstances, extracting what sarcastic capital he could from his frustrations. In the 1860s, the hypersensitivity of Napoléon III's censors had restricted opportunities for publication considerably, obliging writers like Baudelaire, Banville and Théophile Gautier to concentrate much of their effort on art criticism, because that was where the most abundant opportunities for publication were.

When *Gil Blas* recruited the ex-Parnassians Banville and Silvestre as columnists, therefore, the two writers brought aboard a considerable baggage of earlier frustrations that inevitably colored their contributions, helping to fuel the sarcasm of their satirical work. In June 1882, while he was writing *La Lanterne magique*, Banville was also joined on the staff of *Gil Blas* by their old friend Catulle Mendès, who immediately joined in with the games that Silvestre and Banville were playing, not only in supplying the paper with occasional sarcastic fantasies but often splitting his columns into batches of vignettes, in much the same vein as "fillers" he had earlier provided to his own *Revue fantaisite* and to other periodicals he edited briefly. Mendès had also contributed whimsical short stories to Villiers' *Revue des lettres et des arts* in the 1860s, which Villiers had not hesitant to label "poèmes en prose," and Armand Silvestre had probably had him in mind when using the phrase himself.[1]

The experiments that Banville carried out in the short fiction he adapted to fit his newspaper column were often unsuccessful in commercial terms when reprinted in volumes. The last of the stories published in *Gil Blas* as a *"conte fantastique"* and reprinted as a *conte féerique* describes how he arrived home from an editorial meeting at the paper to find that all the *fées* whose exploits had been featured in the earlier stories had gathered in his study,[2] with the purpose of handing in their

---

1 The *Revue fantaisiste* was closed down in 1862 when Mendès was prosecuted, fined and imprisoned for publishing the script of a play, *Le Roman d'une nuit*, to which the censors took exception, and Mendès seems to have taken aboard the lesson that touchy subjects were best addressed in quasi-allegorical fantastic disguise; at any rate, he continued writing *risqué* fantasies copiously when all his colleagues had made more extensive compromises with the ambient editorial pressure to concentrate on anodyne anecdotal stories, frequently evading that pressure by obtaining editorial positions himself.

2 The *fées* featured in Banville's revisionist *contes de fées* are not those featured in the *contes de fées* developed in the salons of the 1690s by Mademoiselle L'Heritier, Madame d'Aulnoy and the Comtesse de Murat—the imaginative substance of which had been adapted and perverted by Charles Perrault— who were enchantresses modeled on those of Arthurian romance, but the "fairies" featured in British Elizabethan poetry and popularized by William Shakespeare. Unlike the fays of French romance, English fairies were tiny

resignation from his work. That suggests strongly that Banville had received notice from his employers that they did not want any more modernized *contes de fées*, and would far rather he went back to writing *contes pour les femmes*. That was what he eventually did, assiduously, although he did try for some time to smuggle various fantastic elements into the various "sideline" projects he attempted in 1882—including, of course, *La Lanterne magique*. Although no explicit reference is made in the Charpentier text to editorial meetings or *diktats* issued therefrom, it is not improbable that he was soon told that that experiment too, and others running in parallel to it, had run their course and had to be abandoned in favor of orthodox "*camées*" and "*contes pour les femmes*." When the serialization of *La Lanterne magique* ended, Banville immediately began a series of scrupulously desupernaturalized stories of Parisian social life, which he initially headlined *Contes Héroiques*, although it is not at all clear whose heroism he had in mind, or of what it consisted.

That apparent disapproval of Banville's newsprint experiments was not confined to the powers-that-were at *Gil Blas*, who presumably thought, or at least pretended, that they were representing the views of their readers. Although Banville's preface to his *camées* explains that he had omitted his closest friends from the more recent examples, for diplomatic reasons, several of those friends were still included in the series, including Jules-Amédée Barbey-d'Aurevilly, one of his fellow critics, who took the trouble to write a full-length appreciation of his work. Barbey, none of whose friends would ever have described him as "diplomatic," was quite forthright in stating that it had been a mistake for a great literary artist like Banville to get involved with newspapers, and he wrote off the entirety of Banville's newspaper work as a worthless exercise in slum-

---

(although capable of *ad hoc* self-magnification), and thus capable of fitting into a poet's study in thousands.

ming of which he could not approve. Barbey, the great popularizer of "*dandysme*," who usually tried to practice what he preached, loathed bourgeois values even more than Banville, and extended that loathing to bourgeois newspapers, but he was not above slumming himself; he published several items in *Gil Blas* in parallel with *La Lanterne magique*, including a feuilleton novella and an anecdotal short story.

Banville, perhaps the most purist of Romantic poets, and certainly one of the more modest, might well have declined to defend himself against Barbey's charge, while protesting apologetically—as he does in the epilogue to *La Lanterne Magique* in the Charpentier volume—that he had to make a living, but he was also the most disciplined of Romantic poets, and he took his literary experiments very seriously. Orthodox literary history seems to have sided with Barbey, in that *Contes féeriques* and *La Lanterne magique* are now among Banville's most obscure projects, given little critical attention, and the tongue-in-cheek suggestion contained in the *avant-propos* that *La Lanterne magique* would be read, while *Gaspard de la Nuit* and Baudelaire's *poèmes en prose* would not, has been proved wrong, although the "magic lantern slides" must have had a far greater readership in the ephemeral pages of *Gil Blas* than *Gaspard de la Nuit* ever had, and Baudelaire's *poèmes en prose* were probably slow to overtake them. However, Banville's experimental fiction is certainly not without interest, nor is it without merit. Even while slumming, Banville never gave up the innate propriety and ambition of his endeavors. He was not an ostentatious dandy in the fashion of Barbey, but when he had a pen in his hand applying ink to blank paper he retained a sense of style and elegance that few of his contemporaries could match. *La Lanterne Magique* deliberately employs a good deal of Parisian *argot* and colloquial phraseology, but always in a spirit of careful stylish contrast.

The claim made in the preface to the Charpentier *Lanterne magique* does raise an interesting question, however: what is the most appropriate label to attach to its inclusions? The prestige of Baudelaire has ensured that his preferred label for such vignettes, *poèmes en prose*, has become firmly established, despite the deliberate perversity of its oxymoronic character. It was aided in achieving that dominance by Auguste Villiers de l'Isle Adam, who used it as a category description in the contents pages of his *Revue des lettres et des arts* in 1867-8, where he published items under that label by Stéphane Mallarmé, "Louis de Lyvron" (Antoine de L'Estoille), "Judith Walter" (Judith Gautier), Catulle Mendès and others, as well as reprinting the entirety of *Gaspard de la Nuit*, encouraging other editors to use the label and other writers to dabble in the art-form. It was not the only label that might have been adopted, though; Louis Bertrand had called his vignettes "*fantaisies*" and Louis de Lyvron called his "*fusains*" [by analogy with charcoal sketches] before accepting the Baudelairean label, thus raising from the very beginning the question of whether such vignettes really warranted oxymoronic description as "poems in prose."

In fact, most of Bertrand's vignettes have little resemblance to poems, and if Baudelaire had not already been accepted as a great poet by the relevant commentators it might have been difficult for them to take seriously his claim that his prose pieces also qualified as poems of a sort rather than short essays or fictitious anecdotes—including some farcical ones. Bertrand's "*fantaisies*" are represented in the title of his collection as being "in the manner of Rembrandt and Callot": a deliberately oxymoronic combination, Jacques Callot being best-known as a grotesque caricaturist—so Armand Silvestre's representation of his "*petits poèmes en prose*" as "farces" is not out of keeping with previous endeavors, although that Janus-like feature of the genre is sometimes de-emphasized by critical commentaries on the nature and history of poems in prose, and many practitioners of the art-form have only worked in deadly earnest.

The question of characterizing "poems in prose" was further complicated by another major contribution to the establishment of the label, made by Joris-Karl Huysmans—not so much as a practitioner, although his collection *Le drageoir aux épices* (1874) can be recognized retrospectively as an important contribution to the genre—but because Jean Des Esseintes, the unremittingly perverse protagonist of his classic novel *À rebours* (1884), has an entire chapter of his character-description given to the observation that *poèmes en prose* are his favorite reading-matter, contending that they represent "the osmazome of literature." Théodore de Banville surely knew Huysmans—he knew everyone in the Parisian literary community—but he did not include a portrait of him in his *camées*. He had not had a chance, in 1882, to read *À rebours* and was, therefore, unable to take advantage of its publicity, but that is probably not the only reason why he did not use the label *poèmes en prose* in *La Lanterne magique*, save for one passing reference to Baudelaire. Although he distinguished its contents from his *camées*, Banville still used an analogy likening them to visual images rather than poems, as Louis Bertrand and Louis de Lyvron had done, and as Huysmans was later to do in *Croquis Parisiens* (1886; tr. as *Parisian Sketches*), in choosing to title his collection *La Lanterne magique*—and, in fact, many of the inclusions do not seem very "poetic."

Gil Blas was not the only humorous paper to make use of ultra-short fiction in the early 1880s, *Le Chat Noir*, the newspaper launched by Rodolphe Salis, the proprietor of the literary café of the same name, similarly aimed for a measure of respectability in its satire akin to that cultivated by *Gil Blas*. Salis invited Émile Goudeau to resurrect his literary drinking club, the Hydropathes, in his café, and to formulate a kind of cabaret there modeled on the performances that Villiers de l'Isle

Adam had organized in the 1860s for *soirées* hosted by Nina de Villard, in which Jean Richepin had allegedly participated, as he certainly did in the Chat Noir, singing his own songs. *Le Chat Noir*'s principal writers of fiction in 1882 were George Auriol and Alphonse Allais, but the paper also reprinted vignettes by Charles Cros and—more significantly—Stéphane Mallarmé, who had not hesitated to call such works "*poèmes in prose*". The cabaret's first resident piano player, Albert Tinchant, also became a prolific writer of *poèmes en prose*, most of which were not humorous, but distinctly lachrymose. For several years, between 1880 and 1885, *Le Chat Noir* and *Gil Blas* were running humorous fiction in parallel, and although the papers were different in their range, and not entirely similar in their style and manner, their endeavors overlapped; it was in a context partly defined by that overlap that Banville's columns, especially the items making up *La Lanterne magique*, appeared.

Given that coincidence of endeavor, it is perhaps not surprising that Banville's vignettes often bear more resemblance to jokes than to poems, but nor is it surprising that they are jokes of a particularly and peculiarly sophisticated kind, which delight in an ostentatious and *recherché* paradoxicality. The very idea of poems in prose is, of course, deliberately paradoxical, and that is why Baudelaire and Villiers de l'Isle Adam, great connoisseurs of paradox and perversity, liked the idea so much. Banville had a different and quieter style, but he was a man of great wit, and when he decided to give his wit full rein, as he often did in the pieces making up *La Lanterne magique*, he could be as flamboyant as anyone. There is no doubt that his work, in this vein especially, is esoteric—arguably far too esoteric for comfortable deployment in a mass-market newspaper—but he was undoubtedly very glad of the opportunities given to him by *Gil Blas*, and he took full advantage of them, while being careful not to test the limits of editorial tolerance too far. Barbey d'Aurevilly did not approve, but it is arguable that Barbey always took himself a trifle too seriously, and he was perhaps not the man most likely to appreciate the finer complexities of sophisticated humor.

At any rate, what Banville attempted to do in carrying forward the cause of Bertrand's and Baudelaire's vignettes in the components of *La Lanterne magique*, was adventurous and bold, and certainly not without influence. Catulle Mendès continued and elaborated his endeavor, and encouraged other members of the stables of writers he assembled for his various editorial projects to do likewise, albeit in careful moderation. The extent to which the vignettes produced for newspapers by Mendès and other writers in the same vein as Banville's *contes féeriques* really qualify as poems in prose rather than short stories, even with respect to the abridged examples that Mendès routinely used to slot into his column three or four at a time, is inevitably dubious, and varies between the other writers who joined in with the game, but the difficulty of classifying such items as those in *La Lanterne magique* is perhaps a part of their charm rather than a fault. They are, in a sense, "neither fish nor fowl" in proverbial parlance, but they might still qualify as "good red herring," and are no worse for that. As jokes they are definitely quirky, and perhaps they were out of place in *Gil Blas*—but they and their counterparts in *Le Chat Noir* certainly played a part in preparing the way for the development of surrealism, and the brief cross-fertilization of ideas and methods between the writers for the two papers did produce a measure of hybrid vigor.

The precise timing of the publication of Banville's vignettes in *Gil Blas* was also significant with respect to the foundation of other periodicals. As well as being prior to the publication of *À rebours*, *La Lanterne magique* was also in advance of the genesis in 1883 of *Lutèce*, the first literary periodical explicitly dedicated to the promotion of the Symbolist Movement hatched in the crucible of Stéphane Mallarmé's *mardis*, his salon-cum-writers'-workshop. Mallarmé had been one of the pioneers of labeled *poèmes en prose* in the *Revue des lettres des des arts*, and it is no coincidence that the two co-editors of *Lutèce*, Charles Morice and Léo Trézenik, both became significant writers of vignettes of that kind. Trézenik issued a collection of them under the title *Décadent proses* (1886; tr. as *Decadent Prose Pieces*), the inclusions of which are cynically farcical in a similar fashion to many of the items in Banville's *Lanterne magique*—which makes very elaborate and flamboyant use of the techniques of Symbolism.

The preface to Trézenik's collection quotes articles from *Lutèce* concerning a journalistic controversy that had developed because of attacks leveled against contemporary poets—especially Symbolists—on the grounds that their work was "decadent"; Trézenik's use of the adjective was ironic, but many of the accused followed Baudelaire's example by deliberately misconstruing the insult as a compliment, employing Gautier's famous argument regarding the nature of Baudelaire's "Decadent style"—an argument with which Banville was, of course, in complete sympathy. Trézenik's new label for prose vignettes did not catch on, although it was echoed by Remy de Gourmont in the first of his collections of such items, *Proses moroses* (1894; tr, as *Morose Vignettes*), but the confusion of labels ought not to obscure the fact that the serialization of *La Lanterne magique* in *Gil Blas* must have had a considerable influence of the subsequent endeavors of Morice, Trézenik and Gourmont and hence, indirectly as well as directly, on the proliferation of prose vignettes in 1883 and thereafter.

Banville largely escaped the label of "decadent" that was attached by journalists to many of his contemporaries, although some of his *Gil Blas* colleagues, including Jean Richepin and Mendès, certainly did not, but as a close friend of Baudelaire and Gautier, Banville would have understood perfectly that his own work was thoroughly "decadent" in the stylistic sense, and never more so than in *La Lanterne magique*. Perhaps, in view of that, his work might have been better suited to *Le Chat Noir*, given that Salis' cabaret was where all the Decadent writers hung out in 1882, but *Gil Blas*, having a larger circulation, presumably paid more, and it had a certain extra measure of pretentiousness that suited him. He would undoubtedly have approved wholeheartedly of the endeavor pursued by Morice and Trézenik in launching *Lutéce*, and also the other Symbolist periodicals that followed in its wake, but it is not surprising that he did not switch his primary allegiance to them; he had spent far too much of his long career in the financial doldrums to forsake the newspapers now that he had been admitted to their pages and their purses, and he had, after all, passed the age of sixty; his spirit was still very willing but his flesh was surely a trifle weak.

It is not at all surprising, therefore, that when Catulle Mendès deserted *Gil Blas* in 1888 to go to work for the newly ambitious *L'Écho de Paris*, Banville went with him, along with Richepin and Silvestre; Banville fitted in there just as well, and perhaps better, since the *Écho* was not an innately satirical paper and he was able to extend the range of his experiments—although *Gil Blas* had also expanded the tonal range of its fiction considerably in the later 1880s, most significantly by publishing a good deal of fiction by Émile Zola and Guy de Maupassant, and by 1888 it had become much more similar to the recently-remodeled *Écho* than to *Le Chat Noir*, which had perished by then in the circulation war in which all the Parisian dailies were inevitably caught up. Mendès was not only a far more prolific writer of "poems in prose" than Banville—and, for that matter, Trézenik, Morice or even Remy de Gourmont—but his endeavors in that format were more varied, and he had a far greater influence thanks to his various editorial exploits; but as well as taking influence directly from

Baudelaire and Bertrand, Mendès undoubtedly took a lot from Banville, perhaps more crucially.

La Lanterne magique was, therefore, a product of a rather brief phase in the evolution of Parisian newspaper fiction, and it is certainly one of the most idiosyncratic products of that phase. It was soon left behind by the tide of literary fashion, along with other varieties of *poèmes en prose*, and perhaps it never had a chance of catching that tide on the flow, but within the curious spectrum of poems in prose the project certainly warrants interested attention; its humor, like all humor, is not adapted to all tastes, but its wit is often pointed as well as polished, and is not unduly blunted by its occasional acute sentimentality. There is certainly room to disagree with Barbey d'Aurevilly and to judge the experiment well worthwhile, and by no means unsuccessful in artistic terms; it certainly has the touch of class that Théodore de Banville imported into all his work. Whether or not it is entitled to be considered as one of the classic collections of poems in prose, alongside those by Bertrand, Baudelaire, Huysmans and Remy de Gourmont, is a matter of opinion, but it is certainly a serious contender for such inclusion.

The translations of the principal components of *La Lanterne magique* were made from the copy of the Charpentier edition reproduced on the *wikisource* website, but I have added two items from the *Gil Blas* column omitted from the book version, as "addenda," which were translated from the archive of the newspaper reproduced on the Bibliothèque Nationale's *gallica* website, from the 17 November and 24 November 1882 issues of the paper.

—Brian Stableford, June 2021.

MAGIC LANTERN

PREFACE

Magic Lantern has one great advantage over all other contemporary books, which is that I have written it for people who do not read and do not have time to read—which is to say, for everyone. In fact, what is the measure of the time that one has for reading? Two minutes, at the most: for a husband, the two minutes during which, ready to go out, already having his hat on his head and his thin cane in his hand, he is waiting for Madame to finish buttoning the last buttons of her gloves. As for his wife, the only moment of which she can dispose of favor of literature is the two minutes during which her chambermaid is putting on her stockings—as witness the witty drawing by Georges Rochegrosse at the head of the volume.[1]

Now, my book is, after the *Fantaisies* of Gaspard de la Nuit and Baudelaire's *Poèmes en Prose*, the only one that can be read in two minutes. But the two works that I have just cited are ranked among masterpieces, and disdained in consequence, so I think that my book alone is destined to be read. That is why I have made the decision to put into it everything that exists on earth, in the universe and in the vast infinities, from the Good God all the way to the most futile individuals, in order that modern French people can have a smattering of everything.

---

1 Georges Rochegrosse (1859-1938), who was at the beginning of his career in 1883, was a historical painter by vocation, who made much of his income as an illustrator and what would nowadays be called a "cartoonist." He provided the frontispiece for the Charpetier editon of *Paris vécu* as well as *La Lanterne magique*.

The *Camées Parisiens* that come afterwards have several grave faults. First of all, instead of having taken a quarter of an hour to write, like Oronte with his sonnet,[1] I have spent nearly twenty years on them, with the result that many of my models have changed so much as no longer to be recognizable, while other petty models have become great. Thus, in order to make them more comprehensible now it would have been necessary to put dates on them. But that would be a lack of gallantry toward the ladies, of which I certainly do not want to render myself culpable, and readers, with the aid of ingenious hypotheses, will have to reestablish the dates themselves. On the other hand, another fault of the *Camées* is that there are too few or too many. Originally, I only wanted to reproduce a few curious faces; I continued, perhaps beyond measure, and yet my collection lacks many illustrious Parisians. Among my friends, I have passed over the best, so difficult is it to do something that has common sense.

Such as it is, however, with its faults, its superfluities and its lacunae, I must admit that I cannot forbid myself a certain predilection for this collection. That is, I believe, because I had, in order to bring it to completion, a collaborator who is dearer to me than anything. Habituated to keeping the house neat and tidy, stacking methodically sheets scented with iris, and even arranging with rectitude the books on the bookshelves and sheets of paper for the printer, my good wife has seen me having difficulty writing the *Camées Parisiens*, and with her impeccable housekeeper's instinct she has put a little order into this heap of Eyes, Noses and Mouths, which I tried in vain to rediscover myself. Seeing better than me, having a better memory and a more rapid thought, she has often collected the notes necessary to my petty toil. Sometimes, in order to go more rapidly, she has written a morsel with enthusiasm, so

---

1 Oronte is a character in Molière's *Le Misanthrope*, who recites a parodic sonnet in Act I scene II.

well, in my opinion, that I have kept it intact, without changing a syllable—with the result that, to my great astonishment and great joy, it has taken two of us to finish this frivolous but sometimes amusing task.

Finally, I still love the *Camées* because Théophile Gautier wrote, in his immortal *Notice* placed at the head of Baudelaire's *Oeuvres*, this testimony a thousand times too eulogistic but so sweet to my soul, which I consider as my best entitlement of nobility:

"We find," he says, "in Théodore de Banville's *Camées Parisiens*, one of the dearest and most constant friends of the poet whose loss we deplore, this portrait of youth and, so to speak, *avant la lettre*. Let us permit ourselves to transcribe here these lines of prose, equal in perfection to the most beautiful verse...."[1]

As for *La Comédie Française racontée*, which terminates the volume, all the merit of that opuscule is in its naïve and perfect innocence. It is a little pamphlet, already very old; God grant that it is not too old!

---

1 The first "cameo" in the first of the three 1863-73 volumes is a "portrait" of Baudelaire, then still alive. Banville was closely associated at the time with Gautier as well as Baudelaire, the three of them scraping a living, in the hostile intellectual climate of the Second Empire, as art and theater critics.

TO FEMALE READERS

Forging prose is sometimes not easy,
Do you know that, Parisian beauties?
Deprived of the meter of amorous laws
One is no longer able to tame rebellious words,
And annoyances come in swarms.
Seemingly in coalition against us.
But as we see when you read us
Your eyes shining and your mouths smiling,
All our wishes are suddenly realized
And that alone is worth the trouble of writing.

RAPID TABLEAUX

Trahi deri, traderi, dère; la, la, la, traderi, tradère! Demand the Curiosity! Have the beautiful magic lantern set up in your home; it won't cost you more than fifty-five sous. Until now it has only been the pleasure of children, but I have invented a magic lantern for the usage of adults, which will show you a thousand ingenious and various tableaux for the amusement of parents and the tranquility of children.

Attach a white sheet to your wall, while calling to me though the window, and arrange yourselves very sagely, like the Tuesday spectators at the Comédie Française. I shall come with my apparatus, and then you will have pleasure for your money. You will see the Good God, and Monsieur le Soleil, Madame la Lune, Mesdemoiselles les Étoiles, the King, the Queen, the Gendarme, the Executioner, Morning, Midday, Evening, the Seven Deadly Sins, the Elements and many figures of an enticing modernity.

My rapid Tableaux will appear to you, grouped methodically in dozens, in honor of the twelve Apostles, and also the number of syllables contained in the alexandrine line, to which I was much given in the days when I was a poet, before embracing an honorable profession.

But I will explain them to you in prose, quite naively, without economizing my most flamboyant adjectives, any more than an honest journeyman painter spares his ultramarine blue, his antimony yellow and his decorative crimson lake when it is a matter of satisfying good practice.

FIRST DOZEN

I
THE GOOD GOD[1]

Under the portico whose stones are ecstatic light, burned by amour, and whose slightest atom, if it could flee, would blind the mad flock of the Suns, the good God, clad as an emperor, seated on his throne, sees and contemplates Infinities. Beneath his feet the quivering ether unfurls, enhanced by imperceptible sparkling dots, which are the Universe. Nearby are the terrible Angels, who are excited because they can hear laments, sobs and gasps reaching all the way to them.

"Oh, Listen, Lord," says Ananiel. "Those are innumerable worlds dying of old age, frozen or icy. Look at their cadavers, stiffening and dangling their inert tresses desperately."

But scarcely has he spoken than thousands of new worlds are born, awake, grow and flee like joyful children, carried away in the ardent music of the universal Rhythm.

"My servant," the good God says to the angel, "why are you afflicted by that which can renew and repair inexhaustible Life? But tell me, what is that plaintive cry that I hear, like a faint murmur?"

"Lord," says Zadakiel, speaking in his turn, "it is coming from the humble planet, forever blessed, where the divine blood was shed. It's a little child in Moulins (Allier)[2] who wants to have a Polichinelle."

---

1 In the serial version the batch consisting of this item and the next three appeared in the twentieth column, on 20 October 1882, far closer to the end of the series than the beginning. The first batch, in the 26 May issue, began with "Le Bon usurier" (tr. as "The Good Usurer").
2 Banville was born and spent his childhood in Moulins.

"But look, Lord," says Raziel, "on that same earth a ferocious conqueror has devastated realms, destroyed cities and tinted rivers red with blood. He has murdered many people personally, whom he had fed to his lions, and he has crushed cohorts under the feet of his elephants. He leaves behind him disemboweled women with blanched lips, pyramids made of severed heads, field where grass will never grow again, skeletons of burned hamlets and bare roads where there is no longer anything but black ash."

At those words the Angels lower their heads sadly. But as the thought of God has pity on their sadness, and as Time does not exist for them, when they raise their eyes again they see the temples rebuilt, the cities thriving, the gardens in flower, the fields full of ripe wheat, and next to tranquil rivers, mothers giving the breast to their new-born children while the midday sun kisses the foreheads of reapers.

"Messenger," says the good God, "you can see that the evils and disasters are cured, and that no dolor will have cried in vain. But go quickly to inspire good thoughts in the mother of the poor ingenuous creature who was lamenting just now. I really want that little child in Moulins to have his Polichinelle."

II
MONSIEUR LE SOLEIL

In the midst of the dazzle of his radiant furnace Monsieur le Soleil is getting ready to climb into his topaz chariot, the door of which is already open, and whose orange horses, always rearing up, are projecting showers of light and pearls from their nostrils. He is clad as a Roman general, in a yellow breastplate with embossed ornaments, a belt with a broad knot, flamboyant lambrequins with fringes, at the top of which shines a figurine of Hercules, an épée, a cutlass and lion-skin shoes with thick soles, which allow the toes of his bare feet to stick out.

High above his floating wig of flame a ruby laurel is posed, from which long ribbons of pink braid hang down, and his golden face, cut above the lip by a tiny straight moustache, as if drawn with a pen, is framed by a cravat of fiery lace.

A few paces away, in another carriage, the vague profile of an old lady can be seen. Around Monsieur le Soleil the princely and ducal Stars are crowding, and to one side, an old courtier, white hot and writing on his knees, is taking notes. However, the Victorious, the Lightning-Bearer, has seen some of the rutilant lords repressing a rapid smile; he wants to know the reason for that, and he interrogates them.

"I order you to speak frankly," he says to one of them. "What is being said about me in the gazettes?"

"Sire," murmurs the incandescent seigneur, "I dare not. Respect...."

"I have said: 'I want.'"

"Well, Sire, chagrined minds think that, by dint of having illuminated them too brightly, your blinding light renders objects vulgar and paltry, showing their infirmity and ugliness, and that Night, with her tender blue softness, gives things a more penetrating and more intimate charm."

"Good!" says Monsieur le Soleil, setting foot on the step of the carriage, "those are simple romantic ideas, to which the legislature of Parnassus will do justice. And all that would not have happened if Monsieur Racine's excellent theatrical work had continued to be performed regularly."

With those words the carriage door closes again. The princely and ducal Stars mount horses, and soon, all the carriages and cavaliers take flight in furious light, and the cortege is no more than flame and conflagration, except for the large thigh-boots of the coachmen, which appear entirely black in the triumphant glory of the universal blaze.

III
MADAME LA LUNE

Pale and plump, and showing her charming features, quite similar to those of the divine Théophile Gautier, Madame la Lune, half set in an arc in an ebony boat ornamented with plates of tin, lead and yellow brass, and incrustations of nacre and silver, with a very high poop and prow, is sailing on the Lac du Bourget,[1] surrounded by the last lunar poets, chimerical grandchildren of the *bousingots*[2] and the Jeune-Frances. As extraordinary as if they had been strolling on the boulevard costumed as Arlequins, those pale lyricists are rigorously clad in the fashion of 1830, and there are even two or three who are wearing boots with tassels and cloaks in which the wind is engulfed.

They are meditating in fatal poses, and a few ladies of the same epoch appear among them, with mutton-chop sleeves and Medieval headbands, as thin as willows, striving to manifest a little presence but evidently relegated, by the very nature of things, to the floating penumbra of dreams.

By contrast, their celestial Mistress, who has not remained a stranger either to modernity or the Impressionist Movement,

---

1 This is a play on words, The Lac du Bourget is a lake in the French Alps, but Banville also has in mind the writer Paul Bourget (1852-1935) who was making his name as a journalist and literary critic in 1882.
2 The literal meaning of *bousingot* referred to a kind of hat worn by sailors, although it became a slang term for a tavern, especially a riotous one, and was applied contemptuously by Royalists during the reign of Louis-Philippe to refer to young Republican trouble-makers.

is dressed in the Japanese style, in order to flatter recent ideas; her intelligence is a little behind the times but her coquetry is not. Her hair lifted up in front, she is coiffed in a tiara in which brass, pewter, lead, pearls, silver and opals gleam, the languid fires of which are mingled in the most various and the most ingenious combinations, and from which her long jet black hair is escaping, dusted with mica and blue powder. Behind the tiara, from which two large pendants in white jet and pale gold hang down, a long veil of blue gauze descends, with designs forming long and complicated meanders in steel-blue pearls.

Lying on a large dog-skin rug, Madame la Lune wears several satin robes one atop another, the most intimate of which is pearl gray, while the others become increasingly bright, until the outer one, which is blue-white, tightened by a broad pigeon-throat belt, and ornamented by pale metal plaques. Around her neck shines a necklace made with the eyes of owls, and she is shod in little curved-back white leather shoes with silver soles, decorated with yellow leather crescents.

"Ah, Messieurs and dear poets," she says, in a sleepy voice, "the amiable lake, with its feudal castle on a rock and its convent of monks lacks nothing! It's there that Lamartine sang of Elvire.[1] How thin and aerial she must have been to have inspired such melancholy lines, like the moaning of the wind in the plaintive iron strings of an Aeolian harp!"

"Madame," says an Oswald slightly smitten with realism,[2] "it's necessary not to exaggerate. It's reliably said that Elvire was a laundress...."

"Oh!" sighs the lady with the silver brow, with a little moue. "Don't take away my illusions!"

---

1 Alphonse Lamartine's "Le Lac," and other poems in which the character of Elvire (allegedly based on Julie Charles, who died of tuberculosis in 1817 at the age of 33, who was the wife of a physician, not a laundress) is also featured, are classics of Romantic verse.
2 Possibly an annexation of the name of the theologian James Oswald (1703-1793), a member of the so-called "common sense" school.

And immediately, to show that it is perfectly indifferent to her, she laughs, uncovering her little teeth of brilliant opal; she wafts herself with her fan of cygnet feathers, and the reflection of her celestial Pierrot face casts thousands and thousands of silver spangles over the gently-agitated waves, which fringe them with delicate and capricious embroideries.

IV
MESDEMOISELLES LES ÉTOILES

Mesdemoiselles les Étoiles have been to a ball, where they have danced madly all night, and now, while going home through the blue gardens of the ether, they are still dancing, coiffed with a sparkling headband, with their long hair thrown backwards, clad in a vivid diamond cloth, with their while legs quite bare, they are coming back, frolicking cheerfully agitating their breasts, picking pale flowers of gems along the path, and not resigning themselves to walk tranquilly, like sage demoiselles.

No, they are dancing, still dancing. Their innumerable choirs sometimes form the figure of a Ram or a Scorpion, or a Lyre or Balance, or an Archer launching an arrow, or a Fish, or a Peacock, or a Whale, or a Phoenix, or a Crane, and all those figures at once, and the immense scattered necklace never reforms, and all those diamond-studded foreheads light up, blanching the blue immensity.

"Come on," says big Aldebaran to little Procyon. "Hurry up, please. Can't you see, already very close to us, the terrible, frightful Aurora advancing in her red robe, who is soon going to burn the ends of our hair with the pink flame of her torch?"

"Alas," says Procyon, "I've lost one of my crystal slippers and I'm following you as best I can with one foot shod and the other bare."

"What does it matter?" replies the grand demoiselle. "Come quickly, and if necessary, throw your other slipper away into some golden cavern; for if you're not careful, we'll soon be walking in the roses of the morning, all splashed with blood. And what will Monsieur Camille Flammarion say if he still sees us in the sky at the regulation hour when honest Stars ought to be in bed?"

V
THE KING

On the wall of the hall in which young King Michel is presiding over the council, the portraits of his ancestors are framed, all clad in triumphal robes, letting long crimson mantles float behind them, holding scepters in their hands, and wearing crowns ornamented with enormous gems over their long hair. It was thus that they once marched through cities, in order that people could say, on seeing them: "That man is the king!" But in order to conform with modern ideas, Michel is clad in a simple jacket, and, authorizing them to do as he does, he has taken with his ministers the great liberty of smoking a cigarette.

"Sire," says one of the old men, "the whole question is a matter of knowing whether the minister Polonius, assembled here before you, will or will not be replaced by the minister Guildenstern, who cannot obtain a majority in the Chambre. For myself, I do not hesitate to represent humbly to Your Majesty that the minister Polonius is the salvation of the State, as the minister Guildenstern would be its doom."

"My dear Duc," says King Michel, "I do not want my people to be like a beast of burden buckling under the weight of its load and lacerated by strokes of the whip. I want the workers, with the price of their labor, to eat real, uncorrupted meat and to drink wine made with grapes ripened in the sun. I want them to live with their wives and their children in salubrious lodgings through which perfumed air passes, and that hearths of infection should disappear, and that hideous Fever flies away from those destroyed dwellings, and that throughout the rejuvenated city, fountains similar to those of ancient Rome pour out pure and limpid water. Finally, I want the citizen—even if he is a prince!—overwhelmed by superhuman circumstances, abandoned by all, including, alas, the Law, to find the aid of a supreme Justice in addressing himself to his King, who must then decide and speak in the name of God. And, Guildenstern or Polonius, the minister who wants what I want, will be conserved, and the one who does not consent will be broken like glass!"

Thus the council concludes, and as he goes slowly down the pink marble staircase the old minister Leonato says to one of his colleagues:

"In the last war, that man was not only able to lead the corps and cohorts of his army, but he fought with a sword in his hand like a soldier, and we have seen blood flow from a large wound in his forehead."

"Yes," the other responds, "perhaps he can be a King, and perhaps he would be, if he consented to occupy himself with useful things instead of dreaming of chimerical progress and wanting naively to give his subjects happiness!"

VI
THE QUEEN

Queen Beatrice has just been brought her little Laertes, ten years old, who has made his face into a great wound by falling from a tree, and the anxious mother is tenderly washing the cheek of her child with perfumed water.

"Wretched child," she says to him, "do you want to cause my death? Yesterday you were wounded by a foil and today there is this terrible fall. Oh, you don't hesitate to afflict me!"

"It won't amount to anything," says the physician, "with a little rest. Only let monseigneur be put to bed."

But Prince Laertes is kneeling before his mother, whose beautiful white hands he is covering with kisses. Then he gets up and runs toward the door.

"Ah, dear and beloved mother," he says as he flees, "I hope to amuse myself soon with more serious and more murderous games than these. Then I'll lie down on the bare ground more willingly than in a bed, and with God's aid I shall not repose except in the tomb."

Queen Beatrice utters a long sigh, but her attention is soon attracted by her maid of honor, the beautiful Duchesse Hermia, who has been unable to retain a fearful gesture. The Queen joins her at the window and sees her other son, little Prince Roland, who, launched like an arrow through the pathways of the park, is mounted on an untamed black horse with neither saddle nor bit, to whose floating mane his little hands are clinging solidly. Quickly, one of the senior squires has been

"

sent to watch the child. Meanwhile, the pallid Queen faints, and after having made her sit down in an armchair, Duchesse Hermia makes her respire salts.

"Oh, Madame," she says, "let them do it. They're never too bold in their savage ardor, nor too cavalier and soldierly to triumph over all the dangers that menace them."

"Alas," murmurs the Queen sadly, "that they were not born humbly into an obscure life, having nothing before them except the mild accomplishment of a facile duty!"

"But my dear mistress," said Duchesse Hermia, accentuating her pretty little moue, full of grace, which renders all men mad, "just think, Your Majesty, that if Prince Laertes and little Prince Roland had been born in that fashion, they would indubitably have become advocates!"

VII
THE GENDARME

Mounted on his horse, as solid as an elephant, the good gendarme Tortezat is going along gaily at a trot, caressed by a storm wind, without paying any heed to the imminent rain, which will drench his well-bleached shoulder-knots and his yellow harness, as bright as flowers. Nor is he worrying about the bandit Gueule-de-Loup, whom he is going, all alone, to arrest in the mountains, and who will certainly fire a few pistol shots at him, directly at his breast.

One might think that Tortezat's face has been carved with a hatchet. His bizarre nose is not attached to any type; the wind, the rain and the sun have polished his brown skin like reckless tanners, and his rebellious and stiff moustache resembles a horsehair brush. In sum, built like a fortress and shod in enormous boots, Tortezat has no other beauty than that of the Devil, and yet, everyone looks at him without having any desire to laugh, especially those who have seen him take hold of bad lots with his strong fist.

Marching toward a serious danger of death, the worthy gendarme is perfectly cheerful and tranquil, as if he were in his garden, occupied in pruning his dear rose-bushes, for he feels that he is the visible incarnation of the Law, and he possesses the invincible serenity of someone representing an idea. And emerging from the orange-tinted sky, striped with violet and bloody bands, are terrifying allegorical divinities, their mouths open and their hair bristling, allowing their draperies—in which a purely conventional studio hurricane is engulfed—to float around their heads, with their naked swords in hand.

VIII
THE EXECUTIONER

Madame is served, but before sitting down at table, the tranquilly united family is waiting for the soup to cool slightly. Necessarily elegiac, by virtue of the law of contrasts, the executioner Josias, standing before a lectern, is playing on his flute a suite once composed for the worthy Tulou, in imitation of a nightingale. His wife is embroidering tapestry braces in petit point, over which a garland of cornflowers runs, and clad in white, his grown-up daughter Eulalie, whose chestnut hair is raised vertically in rebellious bands, is arranging cut flowers as if in a play at the Gymnase.

At that moment the urgent gallop of a horse is heard, which stops at the door. The three individuals shudder, and the Executioner has suddenly become as pale as a corpse. He goes out and goes downstairs to receive the order; when he comes up again, calm and collected, Madame Josias, knowing that her husband will not be dining, hastily serves him a cold broth. After having drunk it, the Executioner puts on his gloves correctly, plucks up his hat and, having addressed a supreme mute adieu to his wife and his daughter, whose forehead he dares not kiss, he goes to warn his aides, makes his preparations and inspects the wood of justice.

Then he straightens up, in his legitimate pride, for de Maistre[1] has glorified him and he is the man who is desig-

---

1 The philosopher Joseph de Maistre (1753-1821) was an important champion of monarchy and social hierarchy in the post-Revolutionary

nated feudally by the name of a city,[1] like a prince of the blood—which he is, in fact, since the social Law sometimes invents such wordplay, as neat and sanguine as the blade of the guillotine!

Era; a collection of his controversial essays, one of which speaks highly of the merits of fear of punishment, first published in 1821, is reprinted in English translation as *The Executioner*.

1 The royal executioner in charge of the guillotine, Charles-Henri Sanson, who did the job for forty years and executed Louis XVI, before being succeeded by his son and assistant, was familiarly known as "Monsieur de Paris," having inherited the appellation from his uncle, who had been an executioner in Reims.

IX
AIR

"Release all!" the captain of the *Leviathan*, the worthy Delgy, as red-faced as Adam and Eve, has shouted, and all the moorings have been released; and like a bird that hesitates at first and then launches forth into the sky, the giant aerostat has flown over houses, fields and trees with a formidable joy. The passengers are Ogier de Lémincourt, Guy de Vauqueleur—for here, as everywhere, nobility gives and gives of itself—the painter Gariel, who will have the Open Air since he wishes it, and the witty Vens, and a few others, among them the beautiful little Princesse de Cytre, the adorable Laure. People would have paid to have such a traveling companion, but, on the contrary, she has paid a pretty penny for the right to go and measure herself against the stars.

Oh, what an impression of wellbeing, of refreshment and of liberation one obtains when one escapes the ground and its tyrannical conventions so completely and so definitely, and when one can say to oneself, with an ineffable sensuality: "I can breathe!" There is no question of vertigo or sea-sickness; on the contrary, an evidence, a tranquil certainty of being safe, enables the blood to circulate freely in the veins. And what is there to be afraid of? One is only going with the flow, with the current that is bearing you away. Sitting on the light wicker stool, coiffed in a soft plumed hat, looking good in her pale blue satin dress with russet lace, which goes so well with the azure and the clouds, the little princess gazes through her nacre lorgnette and seeks beyond infinity for other infinities. And when she sets the instrument aside and lowers her free eyes, she sees the rivers flowing down below between the hills like slender silver ribbons, the little houses, the monuments, the little trees, which might have been taken from a German toy-box, and the somber and bright greens and blues of florid verdure, like a quilt made of little pieces sewn together.

Where are they, the chorus of her jealous enemy friends and her thousand lovers, even the one whom she nearly loved, and whose vague profile she can now hardy remember? All dispersed, as Monsieur Scribe[1] says. But above all, the beautiful little princess rejoices in the immense Air, which she drinks and savors, which kisses her, tickles her, caresses her, flatters her and envelops her in a calm, silent admiration and in the quiver of the long and distant rhythmic vibration, the mysterious salute of murmurs of adoration and praise!

---

1 The enormously popular playwright Eugène Scribe (1791-1861), of whose works Banville did not entirely approve, regarding them as symptoms of the enbourgeoisement of the theater.

X
EARTH

By virtue of the most legitimate of caprices, Madame Denise Valero is lying in her park, on her back, in the soft grass. In the somber pathways full of birds, roebucks and fearful does are running. It is the hour when the sun is fleeing and the golden sky is filling with pink and violet vapors. The weary Earth sighs; a thousand aromas escape from her refreshed bosom, brooks murmur and babble, and leaves quiver. Her head resting amid the verdure, it seems to the indolent beauty that she can hear sap gushing and circulating, and the thousand wellsprings of life agitating mysteriously.

Yes, like a robust black cow that is going to give the teat to her children, the Earth is occupied in slaking the thirst of the trees, the plants, the hectic grass, the roots, the flowers and everything that emanates from her. Circulating in her lush flesh of an attentive nurse is what will constitute the blood of all beings, and within her what will be cries, songs, sighs, respirations and murmurs, the innumerable voices of things, vegetations and luxuriant solitudes, are already stammering.

The beautiful recumbent young woman is intoxicated by those perfumes, those breaths, that movement of the eternal sap, that awakening of a thousand confused noises; and, at the same time, she feels agitating within her the little soul that wants to be born and live, and she shudders at the kisses that she will give to the cherished being later, similar herself to a fecund Earth.

XI
WATER

As naked as a model at the École de Bon Sens, but, with no possible comparison, being infinitely more beautiful, Hyacinthe Marguerit, her tawny hair undone, is lying in her vast red porphyry bath with sloping sides, which once belonged, it is said, to the unfortunate Poppaea,[1] and which her friend Comte René de Leufroi has brought her from Capri, where he found it in the home of vine-growers. The young woman is playing in transparent and limpid Water—for in Paris, with enough money, one can find anything, even, at a stretch, pure water!—and she is savoring its warm freshness delightedly, which is penetrating all the pores of her skin, and she is admiring the emotional wave that is cradling her, and enveloping her like a light veil.

But that is only a loan for a return, for the Water admires the flawless young body that is delivered to it even more, and it is caressing amorously the flexible neck, the white breast, the heroic arms, the young breast with pink buds, the polished abdomen as flat as that of a virgin, the bold torso, the thighs and legs of a huntress, and the feet with transparent toenails. And when the blonde Hyacinthe raises herself partially and wants to call Mariette in order to get out of the bath, the Water shudders as if a red hot iron had been plunged into it, and in a seething of ennui and regret, it murmurs indistinctly, in a faint voice:

"Not yet!"

---

1 Poppaea Sabina (30-65 A.D.) was the second wife of the Roman Emperor Nero (her third husband), who might or might not have caused her death; she was represented by unreliable Roman historians as a cynical schemer.

XII
FIRE

Jacqueline Mézy is undressed. She has enclosed her hair in a light crimson net and has kept nothing on her but her fine batiste chemise, the embroideries of which represent branches of rose-bushes and myrtles. She has snuffed out the candles; but before climbing into her large open bed she cannot resist the pleasure of sitting in a low plush armchair covered in lace, and warming herself at the resplendent Fire that is the only illumination in the room. She uncovers her charming legs slightly and presents them to the flame, which makes soft and tremulous reflections run over her feet. But soon, she puts on her pretty fur slippers again, and quite motionless, she amuses herself in contemplating the Fire fixedly, where a thousand enchantments are accumulating and unfurling.

Rivers of molten metal are flowing between blue and violet mountains. Above them, red copper arches launch forth proudly, on which Amazons in crimsoned golden armor flex their bows and launch their brazen arrows. Monsters, dragons, lions and red birds are agitating in auroral sheets of conflagration, from which triumphant sheaves of sparks suddenly emerge. In a calm, reddening Tempe,[1] thin salamanders in orange robes dance voluptuously. They enlace one another and mingle, lifting their gracious arms and sending Jacqueline their

---

1 The reference is to the Vale of Tempe, a gorge south of Mount Olympus, between Thessaly and Macedonia, the strategic situation of which caused it to be the site of many battles.

rosy smiles. But while they flee into the paling coral shadows, an infamous old woman, all red, with long nacreous white hair, whose ruby nose, curved over a ruby chin, advances to the very edge of the flame, and, showing her scarlet teeth and her green tongue, she calls out to Jacqueline ferociously:

"Isn't it high time to go to sleep? Or, if you don't want to go to bed, at least make the effort to put on a peignoir—slut!"

SECOND DOZEN

XIII
THE ANGELS

Grander and taller than our minds can imagine them, through the immense ether where infinities pullulate and where groups of universes are like grains of vague dust, three silent Angels hasten their vertiginous course, being charged with carrying important messages. They are mounted on their white horses of light and clad in their armor of scarlet diamond in order to combat, if there is any need, monsters and hydras. They go forth, making comets flee, bumping into bewildered constellations, and moving aside the tresses of suns with their imperious fingers in order to pass. They are Malushiel with the blazing hair, who was the tutor of the prophet Elijah; Saramiel, the buckler of God, and Metator, the greatest of the Cherubim, whose splendid white beard floats all the way to his knees; and in the middle of them the young Angel Uriel is riding. At the gallop of his horse, holding on tight to the mane and bending down, the Angel, having picked up an insignificant little ball on the way, is about to throw it playfully with his hand, still weak, beyond the billions of infinities, but the sage Metator stops his arm.

"Leave that alone," he says to him.

"Oh!" says Uriel, raising his ingenuous eyes, in which profound heavens are engulfed. "Is it useful for something, this little ball?"

"No," says the Messenger, "it serves no great purpose, but leave it anyway. It's the Earth."

XIV
HIGH LIFE[1]

The soirée is perfectly proper. The drawing room, in accordance with convention, is furnished with low seats and ornamented with Japanese bibelots, Sitting here and there, as if they had been sown, the women, dressed in more-or-less authentic Worths,[2] painted nicely for the pleasure of the eyes, and agitating fans decorated in the latest fashion, some of which represent very little and others nothing at all, are worse than hanging Madame Eppler, with whom, at the moment, it is good form to have quarreled. Then they chat about couturiers, the difficulty there is in lodging in spas and the impossibility of finding good domestics. The men are discussing the budget and the international Exhibition of paintings, and smoking with distinction light cigarettes of Turkish tobacco. The master of the house, affable for everyone, compliments the writer on his latest book, the banker on his most recent operation, and praises wittily the latest production at the Théâtre Français, the discreet versification of which pleases him infinitely. But suddenly, a window opens violently and gives passage to an old woman with gray hair, thin and dark, cooked by the years and completely naked, who is flying, mounted on a white broomstick. She descends from her mount and throws herself at the feet of the correct gentleman, with the most excited demonstrations of amour

---

1 In English in the original.
2 The fashion house founded by the designer Charles Frederick Worth (1825-1895), reputedly the pioneer of *haute couture*, and the favorite couturier of Empress Eugénie during the Second Empire.

"What's this, Thieunne Paget?"[1] says Satan (for it is he). "I asked you to put on evening dress and to come in a coupé, like everyone else, for I don't want to shock modern ideas and I desire that from now on our meetings should retain the cachet of good company."

Thieunne Paget makes no response, but with her long fingernails she tickles the master's breast, who calms down and starts to smile, and then to laugh, and finally to laugh so loudly that his black coat cracks and vanishes into smoke. All the guests similarly abandon their borrowed clothing and show themselves in an initial reckless costume. The room is changed into a clearing bathed by somber darkness. The King, crowned with iron, is now seated on his throne; the guests are smoking cigars of incandescent coal and, in the guise of tea, drinking cups of flame.

In the shadow of a sinister rock, witches are cooking in an irritated cauldron, from which sobs emerge, and further away the ball is in full swing, to the sound of motifs borrowed from our best operettas and played simultaneously on a thousand pianos by two thousand pianists.

Sometimes the dancers, in order to rest, remove their heads and put them under their arms, and Thieunne Paget, frightfully naked, whose curly hair has adopted a horizontal pose, launches into a prodigious solo cavalier, bounding and striking the nose of the person facing her, and the scarlet bats that fly out of it, with the tips of her feet.

"Let's go!" says Satan with a sigh, agreeably pampered by two young Witches, one of whom smoothes his hair with a red-hot iron comb while the other has passed her bare arms around his neck. "I can see that this Saturday will pass like all the others! My subjects are very amiable, but I fear that I'll never be able to make veritable socialites of them."

---

1 Thieunne Paget is featured in *Le Sabbat des sorciers* signed "Bourneville et E. Teinturier," published in Paris in 1882, an illustrated popularization of the myth of the witches' sabbat.

XV
SPRING

Little Marguerite de Toiras is walking with her cousin Paul in the vast park where the yellow sunlight is playing and laughing. April has thrown its odorous snow and its pink flowers over the trees; a light breeze is caressing the frail and tender green leaves; the rejuvenated streams seem to be rolling waves born yesterday; the birds are singing with delight; all of nature is prey to a contagious folly of renewal, ecstasizing in sweet and furtive smiles, and silently savoring the adorable hour. Marguerite is thirteen years old. Already tall, like the daughters of her race, she walks with the air of a young queen. Her features are noble in their childish grace, but a thousand roses are casting their crimson folly on her cheeks and the wind is mischievously disturbing the smooth tresses of her chestnut hair.

Paul is already a man; he is fifteen years old. A great reader of poetry, he has learned beautiful phrases from his beloved singers, which evidently relate to his cousin, the only woman who exists for him. All of that he is burning to recite to her, to say to her, and it is also necessary to compare her to the stars, lilies, nightingales, diamonds and the inflamed glory of roses, to everything that is most divine on earth and in the heavens. In order to say everything, as he is departing tomorrow to return to prison, to the abominable college, he has taken his courage in both hands; he has promised himself to make a declaration to Marguerite. Marguerite is waiting for it, she senses clearly that the time has come and that Paul is going to murmur in her ear words not yet heard. That is why both of them have fallen silent with a delectable embarrassment, collecting themselves, she in order to listen and he to speak.

But at that moment, without them having wanted or sought it, their hands encounter one another, pressing one another with an unknown force, and under the electric commotion, both sensing at the same time their blood flowing back toward their hearts, while the stream suddenly raises its murmurous voice and the perfume of the trees in flower envelops them with its sweet and deliriant intoxication, the two bewildered children believe that they are about to die.

XVI
SUMMER

Sheltered from the ardent sun by her scarlet umbrella, Madame Céline Rion is walking on the edge of a large field of ripe wheat that is undulating in the wind like a sea, raising and lowering its golden waves set ablaze by the warm light. In the brilliant pride of her triumphant youth, the delighted stroller is the very image of happy strength. Behind her on the narrow path are her two daughters, Jeanne and Marie, walking, babbling, laughing and picking little flowers, and her two sons, the schoolboys Henri and Jacques, already serious, and her husband, a valiant captain of zouaves, who has the gaiety and the folly of bravery. Madame Céline Rion is as blonde as the wheat, which is hers, and at which she gazes tranquilly with her yellow eyes dotted with golden stars. She is tall, and she advances with a sovereign grace. Health bursts forth in the wild and charming features of her face; and without intending to, a white-haired old peasant who is crossing the path at that moment compares the splendor of her lips to the surge of red poppies that cuts through the ears of wheat and traverses them magnificently with its bloody flowers.

XVII
AUTUMN

Madame Jacqueline de Riberpré has something better than youth; she has the expansive and superb beauty of a queen who, at feasts, holds in a plump white hand the golden cup filled with a generous wine. She is not only desired by all, she is ardently, uniquely adored by one in particular, and all women envy her, with reason, the love of Comte Ogier de Sagrède. It is him, that valiant gentleman of a royal race, who is accompanying her in the orchard overflowing with fruits, where, tyrannized by a skillful artist, the espaliers covered with pears, apples and blushing peaches affect the figures of fans, urns and lyres, bending their pride to the omnipotent caprice of man. Madame de Riberpré is carrying the light basket into which she will put the peaches she is going to pick, and which she wants to select, worthy of being appreciated by the most gluttonous of bishops.

Silent beside her, Comte Ogier admires her, and who would not admire her? Under her low-necked roseate yellow damask dress with large flowers, her opulent forms unfurl their magnificent lines; her bold and pure features have a dominating charm, and the design of her red and fleshy mouth awakens the idea of perfection. Around her robust neck a single string of pearls of an inestimable price complete a strange harmony of whitenesses, and her heavy breasts, more than half of which can be seen, are like the white and flavorsome flesh of lilies.

Suddenly, a ray of sunlight has inundated Madame de Riberpré's noble visage with its flame. A vague, fugitive, imperceptible movement has contracted the comte's eyes, but that movement Jacqueline has surprised, and she feels herself struck by it, like a knife-thrust, full in the heart. For she is certain that in that moment, under the fulgurant clarity, her lover has seen the rare red fibrils that are already staining her upper jaw, and the five or six white hairs, implacable signs of impending old age, that are brutally slipping into her thick, silky black hair.

XVIII
WINTER

Pale, thin and terribly old, but still beautiful—for Time itself cannot deform such august faces—the Duchesse de Galatis is sitting next to a latticed window in a bedroom of the feudal château that Viollet-Leduc[1] has restored so ingeniously, but for which the wind and the rain will soon make a new black chemise. With a dolorous tenderness she gazes at her great-grandson Roland, who, sitting on a tapestry stool, is leafing through a Gothic missal ornamented with miniatures. Will that frail child with flesh as transparent as nacre, whose lips resemble a pale rose and whose hair is like golden vapor live long enough, alas, for his name not to perish?

Then the sad ancestress contemplates, in the distance, the vast, immense, blinding expanse of snow, above which crows are flying, and where the marks left by the paws of wolves can be seen in places. On that sinister white page she rediscovers her past, which is slowly written there again. She gazes at all her relatives laid beneath that pale shroud, her husband, her children and her grandchildren, all dead; then, in the distance, the far distance, she sees again the Amours of her youth, whose little cadavers, unkempt in the snow, are displaying their broken wings and, like lips that are sobbing and lamenting still, their bloody wounds.

---

1 The architect Eugène Viollet-Leduc (1814-1879) restored many prominent Medieval châteaux and monuments damaged during the upheavals of the Fronde and the 1789 Revolution.

XIX
MORNING

Dawn, in a saffron peplum, the splendid Eos born of the morning, hesitates to rip the sky of Paris, obscured by the vapors of so many kitchens, feasts and breaths, and by the thick smoke of black chimneys. However, she finally decides, and the tip of her pink nose shows through the clouds. While a few fiacres, dragged by the phantoms of nags, are still rolling painfully, here comes a squadron of street-sweepers on the boulevard, hideous, dirty and covered in mud, the first to go to work in that great galley where everyone will soon be toiling, even and especially the people who don't do anything. A group of young male and female beings emerge from the Maison d'Or. They walk for a moment before climbing into carriages, because they have the pretention of respiring a little air—and what air! The gracious Clérice, who is with them, spots a young sweeper with her hair in a kerchief and a woolen pullover, sheathed in a heap of gross rags, but of an unexpected beauty, with big blue eyes, as white as a star.

"Hey, look at that," she says, showing the girl to little Cursol. "That permits herself to have a face!"

The sweeper has interrupted her work, and leans both her hands on her implement, in a pose full of nobility.

"You know," she says to Clérice, "if each of us resumed her true place, I'd make a very good whore, but it would be necessary to see how you would sweep!"

XX
MIDDAY

Having got up at six o'clock in the morning, Delphine Sitter immediately ran into the depths of the Faubourg Saint-Antoine, to the upholsterers. She has received a volley of insults. She has begged, argued, invented stories, explained theories. They both tore up the bills; she has signed others, and also bills of settlement, and finally she has made up time! From there she flew to the Latin Quarter, and spent an hour of intoxicating amour with the child for whom she is a married woman, stealing those rare instants with great difficulty, and she has fled, reddened by kisses and moistened by tears.

Then she went to see the terrible usurer Martar, and there, at the price of a thousand degradations and a thousand supplications (not counting the ones that she did not admit to herself) she obtained a respite of a few days for the debts of her lover. Lieutenant Georges de Cazeil, who leads his life as he leads his women, and whom it is necessary to save incessantly from all catastrophes. Then, a session at the couturier's and the corset-makers, where Delphine has put everything in disarray, cut cloth herself and cried like a Fury, for she is putting on weight and it is necessary to be thin, and those sluts of seamstresses don't understand anything. Having arrived home at the moment when the fiery sun is launching his burning golden arrows through the gaps in the curtains, she scarcely has time to undress and throw herself into bed, graciously remade and unmade again by the soubrette Léonide, who immediately introduces Jaix, the serious friend, and she offers that speculator the feast of a jolly awakening with the birds.

"Ah, idler," says the enticed Jaix, "you've only just woken up!"

"Yes," responds the indolent beauty, "when you're not here I'm so bored that I prefer to sleep."

"Then I've done well to work for you," he says, timidly offering her a little white portfolio around which golden lace is figured, and which, apart from the banknotes of which it is full, would still have some merit as leather-work.

"Oh," murmurs Delphine, in a reproachful tone, "more money! Don't you know, my friend, that everything except your love is nothing to me?"

For, in order to be swallowed without difficulty, those sorts of absurdities have to be as stupid as the cry of a goose and as neat as the blow of a sledgehammer wielded by a Sioux Indian.

XXI
AFTERNOON

The horsewoman Maria finally appears, mounted on her black horse Selim, in the pathway between the green lawns, where the chestnut trees and trees of Judea are in flower.

Immediately, among the carriages and the cavalcades there is a great movement of curiosity, for no one is unaware that yesterday, the same Maria was left spectacularly by the Comte de Castres, and that the young gentleman in question is to marry Mademoiselle Diane de Sansac. Woe betide the horsewoman if she is sad or distressed, or uncertain; if she has red eyes or if the gaiety of her gaze might have led her to be accused of effrontery. But no, forming an irreproachable group with her fine svelte horse with muscles of steel, well-booted, tight in her riding costume, which falls straight with sculptural pleats, neither sad not cheerful, but serious, with no pallor on her suntanned face framed by short smooth black hair, her eyes bright and full of bravery, the lovely young woman is flying, carried by Selim, who obeys her thought even better than the movement of her delicate fingers. At the same moment, Madame de Sansac's caleche passes; and, although very pretty, during the moment at which she crosses her rival's path, the blonde Diane is effaced, so to speak, and it seems that her rosy complexion fades and is decomposed.

"Well," says Vicomte Ogier de Roye, indicating the scene to Louis de Tende, "I believe that Monsieur de Castres has left the prey for the shadow!"

"Eh!" says Monsieur de Tende. "Reconciling physiology with the old armorial was the dream of Napoléon; but the rest of us, for the honor of a name, have to swallow everything, even dreary blondes, for we're not here to amuse ourselves."

XXIII
EVENING

Alice has just concluded her prayers. She has undressed and climbed into her little white bed, and while awaiting slumber, she dreams. Her soul is like her body of snow and lilies, but as her mother has received many visitors during the day, the stupidities and commonplaces that those bourgeois have pronounced are battling and jostling in her poor little infantile head. However, all that has been seen by her guardian Angel with the beautiful hair. He arrives, invisible for her, and with a light breath, vaporizes, expels and reduces to nothingness that heap of absurd things. Lifting up for Alix a shred of celestial azure, he shows her a corner of Paradise, the blue shadows penetrated by light, the rivers of liquid diamond, the tall forests of lilies, the transparent pink palaces, the bridges constructed with golden rocks where the divine archers stand watch and the flocks of souls in the quivering whiteness of the vast ethers, and, her blood gently caressed and refreshed, the young girl goes to sleep amid those charming visions, in a delectable tranquility.

XXVIII
NIGHT

It isn't a supper, it's an orgy. For Jousse, Zele, Louis de Féry and Diernst of the rosette of a thousand colors have emerged from the gambling den with heaps of gold, and being in haste to finish with that ill-gotten booty they have annexed the most reckless demoiselles, Séraphine, Épine-Vinette and Louise Tambour, and in the private room of the cabaret they are engaged in running up an expensive bill. The most naïve immodesty presides over that feast; hair undone and dresses open, the young women are making epileptic speeches. Everyone is drinking wines alcoholized for the English, eating lobsters spicy enough to revive a dead man or kill a revenant, and getting drunk on perfumed flesh that seems to have been served with all the rest. A storm of dementia envelops them.

Only two stupefied individuals have remained outside the movement. Firstly there is Madame Florentin, that fine colossus who has not understood anything at all since she has been in the world and whose phrases entangle *whos* and *whats* numerous enough to recall those of King Louis Philippe. Then there is the petty artist Joseph Ador, who plays Tantalus naturally and, having never had anything, desires everything. Zele has picked him up on the way while he was dreaming on the boulevard at two o'clock in the morning with an empty stomach. Young Ador, however, has done little harm to the victuals, occupied as he was in swallowing Madame Florentin with his eyes. But at the moment when, out of playfulness or delirium, Épine-Vinette, having climbed on to the table, blows out all the candles except one, when the head becomes a melee in which the devil would not recognize his children, the child rushes toward the enormous woman like a Vandal, knocks her down and grabs her hair, as if he wanted to tear her apart and devour her.

"Wait a minute!" says Madame Florentin, quite tranquilly, who is trying to recognize her cruel conqueror by the vague light of a single candle. "Hang on, wasn't it you that I met at little Célina's, and who promised me two tickets for the Hippodrome?"

XXIV
AN ENCOUNTER

Under the bright rays of the moon, in the plain of Attica, where the pink and violet hills are quivering gently, on a track where some of the rails are pure gold and others electrum, the Train of the Gods passes with vertiginous rapidity, and a poet who happens to be there (those diabolical fellows get in everywhere!) sees, fleetingly, the ruddy smoke of the silver locomotive ornamented with enormous cabochons, where brown Cylopes, forgers of lightning, are stoking the furnace, and the wagons, covered externally with paintings representing the story of Psyche and the amours of Aphrodite. The poet regrets bitterly that the vision has to vanish so soon, but his dread is fortunately deceived, for he hears the messenger Hermes crying in a melodious voice of thunder: "Buffet! Ten-minute halt!"

There is neither a city not a village, but into the air, borne by the wind, the odorous smoke of a sacrifice rises, and a buffet carved from the purest Pentelic marble, painted in bright colors and ornamented with metal plaques, is set up in the shadow of olive-trees and somber carobs, reposing on a golden pavement and illuminated by a thousand torches held by nymphs and satyresses with caprine feet. The Gods and Goddesses come to sit down at tables dressed for their thirst and their hunger, clad in garments similar to those they wore in olden days but tailored in the finest silk and the most beautiful Oriental fabrics, for, even though it is bound to annoy Sardou and the shade of Duponchet,[1] they have broken with wool as well as "holy muslin." Aphrodite's robe is made of a delightful Chinese fabric the color of tea-rose, on which embroideries and heavy silver fringes shine flamboyantly; her gorgerin and the broad belt that clutches her waist are composed of all the various golds and all the dazzling gems. Athene's breastplate is fastened over a skirt the color of marine algae embroidered with black pearls, and even Ares is wearing flexible green armor docile to his movements, like that which Michelangelo has given to Lorenzo de Medici. As for King Zeus, he is clad in scarlet, vermilion and crimson silks, which sing the entire symphony of redness on his divine body.

Although they have kept up to date with modern progress, the immortals, who possess a pure and etheric blood, have not changed their nourishment at all, and have to be content with celestial ambrosia, but with respect to beverages they have not imposed the same reserve upon themselves. Thus, it is iced champagne that the goddesses are drinking from their muslin glasses, while young Ganymede, naked for the pleasure of the eyes, pours King Zeus authentic Johannisberg. Finally—O joy!—the Olympians are chatting in French, and it is also in French that the aede playing the cithara sings, and recites an excellent ode by Théophile Gautier. Of course, as is perfectly understandable, it has been set to music by a Greek musician.

The poet who has slipped in there trembles at every moment lest he be discovered and thrown out like a vile fairground performer; but no one sees him, so thin and emaciated is he, reduced to his simplest expression, the last volume of verse that he published only having brought him relatively insignificant sums.

---

1 The references are to the dramatist Victorin Sardou (1831-1908) and a certain M. Duponchet who was once director of the Paris Opéra.

THIRD DOZEN

XXV
SIGHT

The celebrated thief known among his companions as Tête-de-Loup and in elegant circles as Louis Spéver, has introduced himself into the garden of the town house and all the way to the bedroom of the Duchesse de Segny. Thanks to his numerous talents he has been able to open the shutter; his accomplices are waiting for him down below and here he is, two paces from the beautiful Diane's bed.

His police—for he has spies everywhere—have told him that Madame de Segny has the caprice of sleeping with her jewels displayed around her, and the information was accurate, for the thief admires, thrown on the precious marbles and the plush shelf-units, overflowing their caskets, rare pearl necklaces, enamels, bracelets, streams of diamonds, sapphires and topazes, antiques cameos, Greek and Byzantine jewels, amethysts and corals, all the fiery and crazy flow of an ocean of metal and gems, which, under the sole gleam of a pale night-light, is shining with a thousand and divine fires.

Tête-de-Loup is about to take surreptitious possession of those treasures when something like a crimson glint enters the corner of his eye. He turns his head and looks: O celestial vision! Under the slightly-unmade covers Diane is asleep, calm, peaceful and laughing, clad only in her transparent chemise, and the chemise is open, exposing the most beautiful breasts, young, firm and pointed, ideally pure and perfect in their form, of a living whiteness, with little blue veins and tenderly blushing buds, like those of fresh roses.

Thinking, rightly, that no riches can be worth as much as that marvelous spectacle, and that having been able to contemplate it is royal recompense for his trouble, the thief puts the jewels back in their place, and even adds to them, taking from his finger an emerald of inestimable price that he had stolen recently from the heir to one of the finest thrones in Europe. And he goes back down the rope-ladder attached to the window, still open, taking away in his dark eyes a dazzlement that, under the distant skies to which the judges will not fail to send him one of these days, will console him for everything, even the desperate moaning of the sea.

XXVI
TASTE

The worthy curé Bilco is shivering with terror and alarm as he receives his bishop, Monseigneur Hilaire, who is traveling without pomp in order to bring consolation and aid into the flood-ravaged region, and who has come to request breakfast from him, Bilco! They have been strolling for an hour in the humble little garden where the sun is kissing and caressing giant pears and heavy red peaches, which might have given the maidservant time to make her petty preparations. But in the end, the fatal moment arrives; it is necessary to go back into the house. The table is set up and the tablecloth laid out; in the bottles a wine the color of onion-skin is laughing, and all the bright colors of the faience plates decorated with cockerels are shining merrily.

"Ah, Monseigneur," says the tremulous curé, "I'm too poor to receive Your Holiness decently!"

"It's only food," says the bishop, gaily. "There's the wherewithal here to make an omelet!"

"Yes," responds old Maguelonne, also stupefied, who has just appeared. holding a nice pale yellow enameled earthenware pie-dish. "An omelet, that's all, and this woodcock pâté, made in the local style and cooked in our poor oven!"

She places her pie-dish on the table, after having lifted the lid; and on respiring the delicate odor that escapes therefrom, the bishop remains pensive. Meanwhile, he has taken his seat and invited his host to sit down. Maguelonne comes back, bringing the fuming omelet, the portions are soon served on the warm plates.

"By the relics of Saint Polycarpe!" cries Monseigneuir Hilaire, after the first mouthfuls, having never eaten anything so exquisite and delicious. "What is this omelet?"

"Alas," says Maguelonne, ashamed, "it's simply an omelet with crayfish tails and carp roe, over which I've poured a simple *jus* of pheasant and quail."

"We'll be content, then," says the worthy bishop, secretly admiring the ingenuous maidservant, and in a murmur, he adds: "*Sancta simplicitas!*" thus repeating the words pronounced by the martyr who, climbing on to the pyre, saw an old woman with a child-like soul painfully bringing her poor faggot to enliven the flames.

XXVII
SMELL

The tall and svelte Jeanne has just left.[1] Sitting in a large arm-chair, the immobile poet is dreaming. Soon, his dream takes him over the vast sea; he sees rigging and slender masts in an intensely blue sky, he hears the cries of sailors; joyfully, he sniffs the breeze impregnated with the odor of tar. The ship that is carrying him cleaves the green waves splashed with gold gloriously. Enveloped by warm air, the passes close to green isles, from which heady perfumes of musk, pepper and vanilla arrive; the poet savors those suave odors and is intoxicated by them in respiring the breath that was recently mingled with the air of his bedroom, and the hair of his black beloved!

---

1 The reference is presumably to Jeanne Duval, Charles Baudelaire's mistress and the inspiration of many of his most famous poems, including some in prose.

XXVIII
TOUCH

Someone has knocked discreetly on the door of the dressing room, and Lise Jolia has certainly assumed that the someone in question was her dresser, for she has responded: "Come in!"—with the consequence that at the moment when the amiable dramatic author Lucien Arg does indeed come in, he finds the young actress in the initial costume of an Eve who has not yet put on her fig-leaf: a very simple adventure, the costume that Lise is going to put on soon only consisting of a chemise. As a Parisian, astonished by nothing, Arg sits down tranquilly, and with a perfect serenity, chats about *La Tour de Nesle* and Egyptian affairs.

Meanwhile, slightly humiliated and wounded by not even having heard an "Oh!" of surprise and admiration, Mademoiselle Jolia feels her modesty awaken, bruised, and makes the decision to blush all the way to her beautiful arched eyebrows. Lucien can see clearly that neutrality is not permitted to him, that he ought to execute, or at least lay down, a fortunate madrigal, and as the actress murmurs, folding her arms coquettishly over her bosom: "Oh! I thought it was Adèle. But in truth, what must you think of this… lack of clothing?" the author says, hypocritically, doing his best to imitate the polished and impertinent gesture of Tartuffe: "The fabric is soft."

XXIX
HEARING

The voluptuous Jacques Fabry is lying on his silk divan embroidered with adorably pale colors. He is smoking Oriental tobacco in his long pipe and, from time to time, drinking mouthfuls of a beverage refreshed by snow. In the bedroom ornamented with playthings and amusing objects, forty candles are lit and the fire in the hearth is throwing up brilliant flames. It is the beautiful Laure who had disposed everything as desired, in order that her lover has what he desires close at hand, and seeing him perfectly happy she kisses him again on the lips, in order that he feels loved. Then Jacques picks up the volume of *Émaux et Camées*, open at the page where the *Clair de lune sentimental* begins, and holds it out to his friend.

"Read this to me," he says, "as stupidly as you can, like a newspaper, and without anything recalling the subtle intelligence of actors."

Laure obeys, and in her masculine, pure, adorably sonorous voice, caressant and rich, reads as stupidly as she can the lines of the great Théophile Gautier:

Through the reckless tide
That San Marco sends to the Lido.
A scale rises in crescendo
Like a jet of water in moonlight.

With the air played in a jesting tone
Shaking its bells in the wind,
A regret, a dove that is stifled,
Mingles its sobs momentarily.

"Oh, dear soul!" murmurs Jacques Fabry in a low voice, and, enveloping the calm beloved with his gaze, he feels, running through his entire being all the way to the roots of his hair, enjoyments that penetrate him with the ecstasy of the only truth: Music!

XXX
AVARICE

More beautiful than Goddesses and the ideal creatures evoked by genius, the magnificent Estelle Violas appears on foot on the boulevard holding a scarlet umbrella in her hand, and immediately, Paris, which seemed stupidly dull and tedious, becomes splendid! It is as if, suddenly ripping up the pale clouds, the sun had thrown waves of its golden dust, animating and illuminating everything under the radiance of that gaze and those superb lips. The trees are revived, the window-displays of the shops are amusing, the men appear witty and the costumes of the women recover their brightness, like dull paintings over which a damp sponge has been passed.

The pavement, the walls, the carriages, the passers-by, the iron benches and the kiosks are inundated with joy; the cab-horses launch forward, quivering like the steeds of Achilles, and strolling bourgeois couples sense Amour, long dead, awaken and resuscitate in their aged souls.

Estelle Violas sees quite clearly how happy the ecstatic city is to see her pass by, but, for precisely that reason, it displeases her that beings and things are savoring such delights gratuitously, without loosening their purse-strings, and, like Paganini putting a muffler on his violin in order not to be heard for nothing, she cruelly lowers her veil, reforging in her wake darkness, sad weary hearts and a dull, gray atmosphere.

XXXI
ENVY

Sitting beside her lover, the young Vicomte Paul de Novis, Emmanuelle Manny goes along the high street of Viroflay in an uncovered caleche. She is beautiful, pretty and amorous, clad in a spring dress, young, as a woman is able to be for whom nature and art have no more secrets, made up so expertly that the redness of her blood and the perfumer's rouge mingle in a single and truly roseate hue, and so well-corseted that she gives the impression of not being. She is happy, sensing herself adored by the charming young man who is drinking her with his gaze; but at that moment she sees a disheveled little girl in rags sitting on the ground picking up pieces of broken glass from the gutter, kissed ferociously by the sun.

Bitten in the heart, Emmanuelle, on seeing the beautiful cheeks of that savage child, understands that her own cheeks must seem now what they are in fact: powdered and painted. However, a new spectacle makes her think differently. She gives the coachman an order to stop, and negligently says to Paul de Novis:

"Wait for me a moment; I want to give some money to that pauperess."

And Emmanuelle goes straight to the little girl, whose chemise of coarse brown cloth allows a hole to be seen on the breast as neat as if it had been made by a punch.

"My child," says the beautiful lady, "what made that hole in your chemise?"

Pulling down the coarse fabric and showing her young breast, as hard and golden as copper, the child says: "That, Madame!"

"Ah," groans the furious Emmanuelle, keeping an eye on Paul—who, fortunately, has not seen anything. And before climbing back into the carriage, she gives the little vagabond a louis, and at the same time she pinches her arm with a furious hatred, drawing blood.

XXXII
GLUTTONY

In order to accomplish his sacerdocy, Brumaque has not wanted servants or valets around him. Surrounded by shelves, on which bottles and vessels have been neatly arranged, he will not be troubled by anyone in the exercise of his delicate functions. He has even wanted his meals to be quite cold, in order that no interval will come to depress his pleasures. He has already poured into two of his glasses, to begin with, Loka and white Sicily, and, comfortably seated before the enormous table, where, on a cloth as white as snow, freshwater trout and Loire carp cooked in red wine with its eggs, the duck pâté of the great Tivollier,[1] quail terrine, truffle salad, crayfish cooked *à la Lorraine*, black grapes, peaches with velvety flesh and berberis jam are tickling his eyes agreeably, he is getting ready to proceed when, entering through the cracks in the door, a suave odor, delicious and irresistible, solicits his nostrils and makes his mouth water.

Brumaque gets up, traverses the corridor, and, still following the odorous trail, arrives in his own kitchen. O joy! The cook, Sophie, is not there, having gone out for a moment. With a feverish hand the dilettante uncovers the saucepan, from which the enticing perfume is emerging, and then—immortal gods!—he sees the dish. It is one of those dishes that the artiste executes for herself and never for her master: a mutton stew,

---

1 The restaurateur Auguste Tivollier opened his Parisian establishment in 1854.

but ideal, wild, gilded, with a transparent and warm sauce, and potatoes like living topazes.

Trembling like the thief he is, Brumaque serves that stew with care, and then eats it, tasting it and savoring it, devouring it, so completely that the plate is wiped, licked, washed and cleaned better than by a dog. But the terrified Sophie returns, and, furious, putting her hands on her hips, she says:

"You've guzzled my grub!"

"Well," says the master, pale and trying to smile, "You can take mine."

"All right, for this time," says the cook, severely, "but don't do it again—because I don't eat your filthy stuff myself!"

XXXIII
PRIDE

That Mariette, so terrible and indomitable, who refuses every-thing and wants neither king nor master, and slips between your fingers like an eel, and who draws a knife over nothing at all, Monsieur Adolphe has promised to show to his colleagues, Monsieur Alexandre and Monsieur Eugène, submissive and reduced, as supple as a glove.

In fact, those artistes have gathered in the home of their doyen, smoking while drinking eau-de-vie. Ordinarily correct, clad as gentlemen and coiffed with the most irreproachable English hats, Monsieur Adolphe, for this solemnity, has donned the picturesque costume and mythical headgear like a dignitary who puts on his official uniform for some important circumstance. With his hand he signals that the moment has come, and, taking a silver whistle from his pocket, he summons Mariette.

The tall young woman appears, her eyes lowered humbly, with the attitude of someone ready to obey.

"Kiss the master!" says Monsieur Adoplphe.

Immediately, Mariette kneels down and kisses the charmer's hand, who amuses himself by taking hold of her and feeling her teeth, like those of a pet dog.

"Now," he says, "to the kennel!"

Meekly, Mariette goes to lie down on a piece of carpet thrown behind a trunk in the corner of the room, and there she remains still, holding her breath.

"Damn!" murmurs Monsieur Alexandre, pale with admiration. "You're all there!"

"Yes," said Monsieur Adolphe, tranquilly, with the imperious consciousness of his genius. "One knows how to make oneself loved!"

XXXIV
LUST

In quest of extraordinary emotions, the old sadist Picharles is prowling around the Mont-de-Piété in the Rue des Blancs-Manteaux, knowing full well that strange prey ends up there. He is terrible to see in his costume of a perfect dandy, for hyperphysical vices have twisted his mouth into a pale rictus, and on his face, of an unknown color, with which his wig does not consent to associate itself, all trace of beard, eyebrows and eyelashes is suppressed.

A beautiful young woman, elegantly dressed, emerges from the Mont-de-Piété, livid and tottering, her features horribly convulsed. She is holding a hastily-made package, poorly wrapped in newspaper, whose creases and cracks emphasize, without any possible doubt, the screens that it contains. In order not to reconstitute the drama, it would be necessary not even to have read Balzac!

It is evident that the unhappily-married woman has a lover, and that the lover is a gambler, for only gambling makes such ravages, not only on its entitled servant but all those who approach him. The lover has lost; it is necessary to pay or he will die; the desolate woman is in search of money. She has gone to see Gobseck and Gigonnet,[1] whom she has been unable to soften; the Mont-de-Piété has not consented either to lend her a sufficient sum, and, being unable to save the man she adores,

---

1 Gobseck and Gigonnet are money-lenders featured in various volumes of Balzac's *Comédie humaine.*

the unfortunate lover can find nothing better to do than die with him. She is walking at a mad pace, as if she has been stunned by a sledgehammer, but at the moment when she is about to climb back into the fiacre that has brought her, the sadist approaches the door, still open, and looks the woman full in the face with his pale mysterious eyes.

"*I can give you money!*" he says.

XXXV
WRATH

After having beaten her poor little niece Brigitte like plaster, after having bitten and scratched her and bruised her with punches, and having torn out handfuls of her hair, the worthy Madame Lalouette has thrown the thin and emaciated child to the ground, and now she is trampling the body, without wrenching a cry or a plaint from her. Finally, the torturer stops, not sated but a trifle weary, and the child gets up, with an incredible expression of resolution and strength.

"You don't want to, then?" says the old woman. "A middle-aged man, very neat, who'll give us mahogany, a clock, and everything. You exterminate him, night after night, and I scarcely have my bean tobacco and my poor milky coffee. What do you want, then?"

"I want," says Brigitre, "to work and remain honest."

"Honest! Honest!" howls the old woman, drunk with rage. "Decidedly, I have no luck; there's only one of them, and it falls on me. Come on, will you do it?"

"Never!"

"Ah! Never!" vociferates Madame Lalouette, turning crimson. And seizing a cracked pot, which she brandishes, she finally breaks it into pieces on her little victim's meager back.

"Slut!" she says.

XXXVI
SLOTH

Louis Feller is sprawled on a gray silk divan embroidered with pale flowers. On the same divan, not far away, his beautiful mistress Lydie is lying, clad only in a transparent gauze peignoir and her unbound hair. Close by, on a nacre table covered with a soft Persian rug in faded colors, the poet sees united his favorite book by Lecontre de Lisle, all his smoking equipment, cut roses and iced beverages prepared in glasses with drinking-straws. In order to procure any voluptuousness he might choose, he has only to reach out his hand; but he does not reach out. He prefers to bathe in the sonorities of a verse by Baudelaire that is singing in his head and which he will remember soon. And on due reflection, he would like even more not to recall the sweet lines that have flown away, and to do nothing at all, only consenting very feebly... to exist!

FOURTH DOZEN

XXXVII
WINE

In front of a tavern in the old faubourg Saint-Germain, which, by a singular chance, in that quarter whose terrain is nowadays covered with gold, still occupies a single-story house shaded by and clad in the branches and foliage of a centenarian vine-cep, the young Duc Enguerrand de Hély and his friend, the painter Léon Bertrix, are sitting at a little table on which a bottle and two muslin glasses are placed, half-filled with bright crimson red wine, charming to behold—and they are drinking while watching beautiful Parisiennes pass by.

It is one of those spring afternoons when the sun, already hot, makes Paris the most beautiful place in the world, where the nascent foliage and the garden flowers are splashed with gold, and where the women, with their gracious faces and their costumes imagined with genius seen to have reflowered too, like the month of May. For inventive men, to see them glide lightly over the asphalt is to read and spell out a thousand eclogues, a thousand novels and a thousand unexpected odelettes—and the two friends are intoxicating themselves with that amusing and poetic spectacle, while savoring the wine, which is kissing and caressing a wayward sunbeam.

Duc Enguerrand has known the tavern-keeper for a long time; he has been one of his family's servants and, by virtue of a bizarre combination of circumstances, has remained an honest man. The Duc knows him so well that he sells him a part of the crop of his vineyards personally. While passing by,

Bertrix and he felt that they were thirsty and that they would willingly have a rest, and as the Duc was sure of finding at Père Berluque's an excellent and sincere bottle of Mercurey, he has invited his companion to sit down under the antique trellis.

And the Parisiennes in fresh dresses woven by the fays gaze with an admiration mingled with respect at those two young men, as handsome as Amadis, evidently aristocratic enough, elegant and sufficiently dissimilar to the bourgeois to sit down without any embarrassment among worthy laborers, in order to have the right to flee the hideous cardboard cafés where the paltriest of Locustas perpetrates her vulgar crime on a daily basis, and to dare to drink good wine at a wine-merchant's!

XXXVIII
TEA

In Cannes, in the small drawing room of a villa whose open windows permit the sapphire waves of the sea to be seen and heard singing, Miss Amy, Miss Deborah and Miss Eleanor, left alone while their parents attend a grand soirée at the home of Lord Norris, are taking tea to distract themselves, and above all to satisfy their hunger. Oh, the beautiful victuals that are, in fact, laid out on the pictorial Russian tablecloth, where the tea is fuming in China cups ornamented with grim and disquieting monsters! Caviar, galantines, Russian salads, cold poultry, game half-buried in transparent jelly, tongue-paste sandwiches, pheasant pâté, lobster pâté and all other possible pâtés, are crowded there densely for the pleasure of the eyes, in the shadow of a vast ham, the sliced flesh of which is unfurling in harmonious scales an entire symphony in pink.

And rosier still are the three misses. All young, almost still children but tall and lithe, like Rubens nereids, superb and colossal, blushing under their blonde and red hair, whose beautiful flesh, conscientiously nourished on succulent roast beef, inspires the idea of flowers and ripe peaches. Tranquilly, efficiently, without resting for a moment, those fortunate virgins are stuffing themselves with boneless quail, fillets of partridge and infinitely varied sandwiches, and emptying their cups one sip at a time, in which Indian tea is fuming, so delicately and deliciously perfumed, and showing their frightfully white little carnivorous teeth behind crimson lips, chatting about their amours.

"Yes," says Deborah, "I shall love my dear Midshipman Edward Novel forever, for he is tall, like us, white and pink, without a wisp of beard. He looks so much like a girl that in the Polynesian islands a queen wanted to eat him, and the slightest breeze scatters his fine light hair. And you, Eleanor, are you still smitten with your Hungarian pianist?"

"Yes," says Eleanor. "I'm fond of him because of his air of fatality. Music stuns him and bowls him over like a storm wind. When he plays, the sobs of the instrument seem to be emerging from his broken breast, and one might think that he were a piano himself. I'm interested in him because it's incessantly believed that he's going to die, and it's in that regard that I'm very different from my sister Amy; for doubtless, what pleases her in Sir William Sidney is that the lieutenant in the horseguards can strangle a horse between his legs, and bend a gold coin in two with his fingers. But he's not the only one who can accomplish those feats of strength."

"Anyway," says Amy, "it isn't for that reason that I adore him. If I've made him my god, it's because of something else. He'd forbidden me to continue playing the coquette with our cousin Anthony, and as I'd disobeyed him by meeting Anthony alone on the stairs, he gave me a great slap, which threw me into a pure delight, for that's precisely how one loves!"

While speaking thus, Amy raised her eyes to the heavens, and drank another cup of tea with a sweet penetrating perfume, while Miss Deborah and Miss Eleanor stripped and laid as bare as Andromeda the armoried golden plate that contained the chaufroid of warblers.[1]

---

1 *Chaufroid* is a contraction of *chaud-froid* [hot-cold], referring in culinary jargon to a cooked dish intended to be served cold.

XXXIX
COFFEE

All night, the poet Paul Sirvent has been tamed by the victorious Muse, thinking in full, firm and sonorous verse, and imprisoning in rhythm with an agile dexterity the superb, comical and gracious images that are crowding his brain. Next to him, on his table, sheets of paper are piled up, full of lines written without any being crossed out, in a bold and clear handwriting, and he is still writing. But he is tired and wan, and his eyes are burning when dawn arrives, casting its white light through his poorly closed curtains to make his lamplight pale. At that moment, the poet sighs, exhausted by the never-ending and ever-recommencing struggle, almost despairing, although full of the courage of translating, such as he imagines it, pure and serene Beauty. But he feels better, calmed and retempered, as if by a refreshing wave, simply by virtue of seeing Émilie, his dear and faithful wife, come in.

Beautiful and illuminated by amour, clad in a white peignoir, her thick and bushy black hair swept back from her narrow forehead and her eyes full of softness, pride and maternal tenderness, she is holding a cup as white and thin as an eggshell, into which she has poured hot coffee for her beloved laborer, which is exhaling a precious and divine aroma. She has chosen the green beans of that coffee one by one, mixed them in savant proportions, and roasted them herself with minute care, so that they are not blackened and remain delightfully blond. Then she has ground the beans; with her beautiful, elegant hands she has poured over them slowly, at faithfully-observed intervals, pure and limpid water boiled over a bright flame; at the bottom of the cup, before dropping the black liquid into it, she has put a lump of real sugar, obtained by means of the most patient cunning.

And now she is bringing her friend a beverage that all kings would desire in vain, but which is worthy of recompensing the ecstatic vigil of the poet, whose thoughts will fly away into the entire world like birds of joy and light.

XL
GIN

In Fleet Street, at nine o'clock in the evening, in the midst of London's black fog, in which one divines or hears the turbulent crowd without seeing it and the gas-jets burn like bloody flowers, the aged Lord Henry Lilly is approached by a tall tragic woman.

Her eyes are extinct; the pallor of death extends over her bold features; long wisps of white hair fall from her bare cranium, and her neck seems broken, like a wounded snake. She is enveloped in a sinister rag, which must once have been an empty sack, having become beautiful by virtue of horror; her legs are bare and her meager bare feet are paddling in the mud.

"Oh, sir," she says, "I'm cruelly thirsty. You'd be very kind to buy me a glass of gin."

Lord Lilly, who is rich enough and generous enough to satisfy the desires of the whole world, has never refused anyone anything. He goes into a drinking den with the old woman, where the crystal bottles on the sculpted silver counter shine like heaps of diamonds. Prostitutes, jockeys, boxers and pickpockets would gladly have a laugh at the wretched Kitty's expense, but they do not dare because of the lord accompanying her, and she drinks her glass of gin tranquilly. Scarcely has the liquid flame traversed her throat than she seems to be reanimated and reborn.

"Another?" she says, timidly, like an imploring child.

"Yes, another," says the lord, "and as many as you wish."

The old woman drinks several glasses, one after another, and her lips redden, her neck straightens, a gleam appears in her glaucous eyes, and, as if mad with gratitude and joy, she cries: "Ah! Thanks… Thanks, Henry!"

"You know my name?" queries the astonished Lord Lilly.

"Yes," she says. "I was Kitty, little Kitty, chambermaid to your mother the Duchess, in her country house in Berkshire, where the black swans floated on the quivering water of the somber river. And I believe that I was the first girl to whom you said: 'My dear heart.' But many days have gone by since then; I was beautiful, but now I'm ugly, frightfully ugly."

"No," says Lord Lilly, recognizing the companion of his youth, like a funereal Fate, resuscitated by the gin. "It's another kind of beauty, that's all."

XLI
BEER

The celebrated Parisian *soiriste* Sabrazès has taken advantage of the second entr'acte to go and drink a rapid tankard of beer in the only brasserie in the quarter that obtains serious provisions from Munich. It is delightful to gaze at the topaz flood in which the gaslight is reflected; he has drunk it and been refreshed, and now feels better; but unfortunately, he has forgotten—not to bring his pipe. He feels it when he puts his hand in his pocket, and immediately experiences an immense and imperious need not to return to the comedy. He has, worse luck, an excellent dry tobacco; he stuffs his pipe and lights it, and smokes it while drinking another tankard, and then another, and, as my master says in *Le Parricide*:[1]

Another, another, another, another, O funereal heavens!

And that excellent light and nourishing beer renders him absolutely happy. He flees the theater; he will not return to it, the theater, which is good for Sarcey![2] However, it's necessary that the *soiriste* write his *Soirée*; how is he going to do it? But the fay Houblon[3] is no more stupid than another; in the

---

1 "Le parricide" is a section of *La Légende des siècles* by Victor Hugo, but the quoted line does not appear therein.
2 The notoriously conservative theater critic Francisque Sarcey (1827-1899), of whom Banville did not approve.
3 Houblon (*Humulus lupulus*) is a plant in the family of the cannabinaceae, an extract of which has long been used in Bavaria and elsewhere for

flood of immobile gold fringed by blonde foam, she shows the drinker distinctly the pale golden hair of the little actress who is playing the principal role in the play, and then her undine eyes, her slightly tight lips, her nacreous face, and, in sum, all of her child-like and bizarrely pre-Raphaelite person.

Fervently, with his model before his eyes, Sabrazès improvises an excellent portrait of the little actress, which is very close to nature; he embellishes it without difficulty with two or three twists, having learned the principles of inventing anecdotes. Then, having put his copy in his pocket, he empties his glass, swallows everything, beer and ingénue alike, and, now free until midnight, orders another one, which he can drink at his leisure, without any anthropomorphic transposition, simply for love of the beer.

---

flavoring beer.

XLII
THE GOOD USURER

The usurer Ange Aprei is charming. A pretty nascent beard proliferates amusingly around his rosy face. His blond hair is cut in the form of a gridiron. Clad in a satin waistcoat, satin trousers, and a Russian shirt in sparkling silk, shod in cashmere slippers, he gives the impression of being made of sugar, jam and whipped cream, and, his cheeks and lips illuminated by a benevolent smile, he is sitting in an armchair upholstered in cream satin; he is smoking a cigar as blond as he is, which creaks in his fingers, and standing before him is a young man with a tanned face and black hair, all of whose features express a virile resolution.

"Poor dear!" says the delightful Ange. "You want to elope with a woman who adores you, and for that you need a large sum of money; it isn't me who'll refuse you! Let's be modern and call things by their name. I'm a usurer. But we've come a long way since Molière's usurers! I won't tell you that the money will be furnished to me by an obliging woman. No, dear, it's there in my safe, and I have only to extend my hand to get it. Above all, I won't pay you in quilts and stuffed crocodiles. No, money is money; today, it's a matter of simplifying everything. You're going to give me an IOU for forty thousand francs payable a year from now, and I'm going to give you eighteen thousand francs in honest banknotes; you see that I'm brisk in business. No, dear, don't thank me; it's quite simple; either one has friends or one hasn't.

"Only, you'll need a gift for Séraphine. Oh, that won't be difficult, there's no need to search for it. The girl is crazy about sapphires, may the devil take me if I've ever known why. And then, appropriately, you'll send me your Detaille.[1] You know that I've always had a yen for it; and then, the little lieutenant who is charging the Prussians is truly reckless!"

1 Edouard Detaille was an Academic painter famous for his military paintings, who enlisted in the French army during the Franco-Prussian War in quest of realistic images. When the present vignette appeared in *Gil Blas* Detaille had not yet published his classic imagistic study of *L'Armée français* (1885), but Banville had been familiar with his work since the Salon of 1868, in which Detaille first exhibited, in the days when Banville was scraping a living as an art critic.

XLIII
ARTSA

The supper is drawing to an end. The banker Zipper, the poet Charleuf, the great founder of newspapers Michenon, Marquis Avelle, who has just married, and the rich feather-dealer Barriol, his father-in-law, are all drunk, and as loquacious as thrushes in a vine. The tall Aurélie has let down her hair, the slender Josephe, in a red dress, is eating a rose, and one can see the young breasts of Nini Plumet through the gap in her dress. The flames of the candelabras, the silverware and the champagne in crystal decanters also give the impression of being drunk, and in the vases large poppies are bleeding like severed heads. The noisy and absurd chatter mingles with the sound of kisses, and by virtue of a horrible prodigy, the composer Girolet, sitting at the piano, is weaving together Sébastien Bach and Charles Lecocq,[1] by means of crazily ingenious transitions. Suddenly, under his feverish fingers, one of the instrument's strings snaps, and a silence falls in which Michenon can be heard saying to Zipper, in an indignant voice:

"No, the Jew Izebel isn't an active partner in my new newspaper, *La Paix définitive*, and I'll never permit anyone to say such things. Me, ask for money from a race that sold the good God!"

---

1 Charles Lecocq (1832-1918), well-known for his comic operas, was at the height of his fame, assured by the great success of *Giroflé-Girofla* (1874)—cited elsewhere in the present volume—when this vignette was written.

"But Monsieur," says the soft voice of the young Israelite painter Artsa, who had been silent until then, occupied as he was with the pink fingernails of Laure Pignoche, "a large enough number of honest men are gathered here, and it seems to me that all the professions we exercise are precisely consistent with selling what ought not to be sold!"

XLIV
TWO POLICHINELLES

Beautiful, cheerful and rosy-cheeked, ravishing with their blonde hair, their silk and velvet garments, their white collarets and their lavishly-knotted broad belts, the children sitting on the benches are watching a comedy, full of an immense joy. The White Cat, as white as snow, bristles his moustache, turned up like that of Captain Matamore, and as for Polichinelle, drunk, excited, delightful and ferocious, he has never been as content as he is today; he is split like a set of compasses; blazing like a firework, his nose gives the impression of a ruby in a furnace, and with his fine trickery he beats and slaps the inexorable Commissaire with whirling arms. *Bang, bang, bang!* He beats his legs, his arms, his cavernous back and his wooden head, knocking him down with furious blows, which make the sonorous garden quiver. O Commissaire, it is in vain that you try to avoid your fate by rapid flight; your enemy always catches up with you, grabs you delightedly and *bang, bang, bang*, continues to administer the heroic beating. And the little children laugh like maniacs, showing their white teeth. But a grave monsieur, who has donned a black coat this morning because he has to go to dinner in town, and who is very annoyed with Polichinelle—even though, with his red face, his white hair and his hooked nose, he resembles Polichinelle perfectly—seething with an indignation that he does not attempt to conceal, cries:

"It's shameful to give children such spectacles! How can one expect them, after that, to respect authority and the representatives of the established order?"

"Oh, Monsieur, says a sage sitting alongside him, "don't trouble the pleasure of children, and let them amuse themselves tranquilly, for the love of God!"

"Hmm! God!" grumbles the Polichinelle in a black coat. "He hasn't conducted himself very well either during his terrestrial life. Is it regular conduct continually to bring his friends to dine in town in the homes of people who haven't invited you, and then pick up on the road a horseshoe that doesn't belong to you, and sell it in order to employ the money to buy cherries?"

XLV
BUSINESS

At the door of the celebrated paper-manufacturer Malpiece—who, like Susse and Giroux, sells in his splendid shops situated on a recently-constructed boulevard, lamps, bronzes, vases, furniture, oil paintings and, in sum, everything except paper—a handcart drawn by a robust man with a graying beard stops. The man goes into the shop and approaches the master of the house timidly, already vanquished by his cold gaze, like that of an ox about to be stunned.

"Well, my dear Sagne," Malpiece says to him in a deliberately disdainful and discouraging tone, "what have you brought me now?"

"It's an item of furniture that I've made entirely by myself, with love, in the mornings, evenings and nights before and after work, in order to try to relieve our poverty. For you know, Monsieur, that I'm very poor and I have six children."

He goes out and comes back immediately, carrying in his arms a piece of furniture in the Louis XIII style, in ebony encrusted with ivory, with delicate silvered bronze ornaments at the corners: a true masterpiece, whose design, proportions and finish are admirable, and whose incrustations have been imagined with the richest and most savant whimsy.

"Pooh," says Malpiece. "What do you expect me to do with that? I've told you a thousand times that you're too artistic and you're searching for the little beast. I don't deny that it's perfection, but who will perceive it? It's a piece of furniture that I might be able to sell but—who can tell?—after having kept for two or three years in the shop; and in the meantime, I'd lose the interest on my funds. However, I don't want you to have come for nothing; I'll give you eight hundred francs for it."

"Oh, Monsieur," says the craftsman, trembling with dolor and anger, "in order for me to earn something from it, if only the price of my time, it would be necessary to pay me two thousand."

"Come on," says the paper-maker severely, "no childishness. If you want, Monsieur Berra will count you out eight hundred francs, but don't say another word. I'm expected, I'm getting into a carriage, and if the matter doesn't suit you, we'll never have any further dealings."

Heartbroken and desperate, Sagne receives his money. At the same moment, a grand seigneur, six times a millionaire, Marquis d'Eveno, comes into the shop. The sales staff and their master hasten toward him obsequiously; even the paper-knives and lampshades seem to want to besiege him with the basest flatteries. Pictures representing women of the Directoire painted blandly and vaporous landscapes for export offer themselves to him cynically, like prostitutes, but he turns a deaf ear and goes straight to Sagne's piece of furniture.

"That," he says to Malpiece, "is a veritably marvelous dresser. Send it to me immediately."

"I can't," says the paper-maker, "let Monsieur the Marquis have it for less than six thousand francs."

The marquis takes six thousand-franc bills from his wallet, hands them to the cashier, and goes out, saying to Malpiece:

"Such an object is never dear!"

The craftsman has remained in his corner, silently. For a moment, the eyes of the Marquis d'Eveno and his have met. The two men have been on the point of making one another's acquaintance, but the voice of the paper-manufacturer has come to break the spell, and the grand seigneur has departed without having divined the great artist. Once he is no longer there, Sagne makes a supreme effort and addresses one last plea to Malpiece.

"Monsieur, he says to him, as pale as a linen sheet, "since the matter has turned out so well for you, let me have two thousand francs—which, I swear to you, are indispensable to me.

"Oh," says the impatient merchant, "you'll never be reasonable, then! When will you finally understand that business is business?"

Then one of those desolate and grim flashes passes through the poor man's eyes that we have seen catching fire in the street in days of civil war, and, burning like molten lead, a tear trickles down his cheek, which would have softened the terrible Angels but cannot disarm the ferocious paper-manufacturer; for commerce is a serious matter, and one does not pay forty thousand francs in rent on the boulevard to let oneself be abused by sentimental nonsense.

XLVI
DANCE-HALL EXIT

Little Julie is very happy. She has just rediscovered, in the Reine-Blanche dance-hall, her childhood friend Céphise, who has remained sage and continued to live on her needle, whereas she, Julie, leads the rude existence of a lost girl, obedient to masters who do not joke. But she has felt comforted and consoled on seeing her dear companion again. She will follow her into her little room, and there, tranquil and serene, forgetting the cruelty of her tyrants, she will sew as before, occupy herself with housework, and sing the old songs with her pretty bird-like voice. The two girls have bought for their supper a punnet of strawberries and a little wine. They go on gaily, laughing, making a thousand plans, walking with a light step in the blue night, and the wind joins in, playing with their hair. But, under the raw light of a gas-jet, they see Monsieur Alexandre coming toward them.

He is serious and dressed, not in the legendary commonplace manner, but in accordance with the most recent fashion customary in the society to which he belongs. He is not wearing a top hat. His elephant-foot trousers, his pointed shoes, his straight collar, his bright cravat, his little hat and his hair, which forms a jagged line over his forehead, inspire respect, and in his chamois gloves with blue seams tucked into his waistcoat he cuts the best figure in the world. Silently, he parts the arms of the two young women; then, without paying any attention to the blushing and stupefied Cephise, and without departing from the calm inseparable from true strength, he says to little Julie, who is trembling like a leaf:

"*Well? To work!*"

XLVII
KINGS IN EXILE

While walking in the Luxembourg, near the fountain, the poet Jean Sézary gazes at the Swan gliding slowly over the calm water and remarks without difficulty that it seems very sad. Soon, although no sound really strikes the air, the poet listens to an internal voice that speaks to him, and has no doubt that the melodious voice is that of the Swan.

"Well, no, my brother," says the great snow-white Bird, raising its head dolorously, "I can't get used to this little green-painted house, to the nursemaids and to this garden of red epaulettes, and the ridiculous simulacra of ships that the children launch so joyfully on the dormant water. For I'm the bird of the gods, born to extend myself, in the shadow of oleanders, over the quivering bosom of Leda; I'm the bird of warrior chiefs, made to glide over a somber river, in front of a château bathed in morning mist. I can't resign myself to being part of this vulgar ensemble, and the cry of the waffle-merchant annoys me particularly, not to mention the statues denuded of style that loom up like marble milestones over the black masses of foliage."

Desolate at being unable to assist the lyrical bird, Sézary leaves the garden, and then, in the Rue de Seine, he stops and contemplates in the window-display of a pork-butcher's shop a beautiful cut Lily standing in a crystal vase. But the flower speaks to him, as the bird had done.

"I am," it says, "the lily of the wild valley, born to be compared to the whiteness of a Bride and the vestment of King Solomon, and I cannot console myself for dying in the midst of these fake *rillettes de Tours* and these *langues de boeuf à l'écarlate*, cooked without *écarlate!*"[1]

"In fact, that Lily is unfortunate," says the poet, who would like, if he could, to console all beings, and, sympathizing with the white Flower and the stainless Bird, he goes to correct his proofs—at the newspaper.

---

1 Recipes for both these traditional French dishes, the former made from mashed pork and the latter from ox-tongue, are still easy to find, nowadays represented as gourmet dishes rather than cheap food for poor folk.

XLVIII
MEDITATION

In the beautiful Louis XIV drawing room of little Savine Miron, the rich financier Linail, exasperated by the long wait, has ripped his gloves into little pieces, and in the rococo drawing room the Prince of Macedonia is chewing his long and fine blond mustache. Savine has forgotten both of them, with an impartial justice, and yet she is not doing anything at all. She is in her boudoir hung with pink Chinese silk embroidered with silver; enveloped in a transparent chemise and her undone hair she is lying on a sofa, her little bare feet posed on the arm of the item of furniture, gazing at a beautiful cut rose placed in a vase facing her, on a nacre-topped table; she is thinking about absolutely nothing, contemplated in her turn by the pale rose with the blushing heart.

FIFTH DOZEN

XLIX
ARISTOCRATS

On a path in the Parc Monceau near a flower-bed of red geraniums, the young captain of hussars Jean de Lesigny is walking with his wife, while his son is carried by a beautiful maidservant. Comte Jean is descended from the Rénier who fought alongside Louis XI at Damiette, with Jean de Beaumont, Mailheu de Marh and Geoffroy de Sargines. From the first Rénier to Guy, Jean's father, who fell at Champigny pierced in the chest by three bullets, the Lesignys have all been soldiers. Our entire history is splashed by their exploits, and they have given so much of their blood that none now remains to them. Under his short golden hair and his thin blond moustache, Comte Jean is as pale and blank as a sheet of paper, and his wife and cousin Éléonor, the daughter of a dying race, is as pale and bloodless as he is. Borne in the arms of a robust Dijonnaise with superb pink cheeks, the white and transient child with effaced features gives the impression of a little phantom. He is trying to cough, but he does not have the strength, and in order to protect his poor weak eyes from the light he has been equipped with dark glasses.

L
AN ACTRESS'S DRESSING-ROOM

At the door of the great tragedienne Tamnâ, General Chanor, intoxicated by rage, has been knocking with his hands and feet, unheeded, for a good quarter of an hour, and proffering atrocious oaths in a low voice. Finally, a chambermaid comes to open the door to him, and the furious general enters the dressing-room as if he is about to murder everyone, but he is stupefied and dazzled by the ingenuous smile of the actress.

Squatting on the floor on the white velvet carpet, Tamnâ is playing a hand of piquet with the great dramaturge Taravant, squatting like her, whose dark eyes, black hair standing up vertically and broad face with scarlet lips express a tranquil joy. As for Tamnâ, who is playing Phèdre tonight, she is dressed in an antique style in red and pink, with a very amusing Japanese robe ornamented with pale gold jewels copied perfectly from those in the Campagna museum. Her pale pink tights mold her legs and the toenails of her small feet very graciously, and while playing cards she is smoking a cigarette of Turkish tobacco.

"Blood and thunder!" howls General Chanor as he comes in.

"Ah! You're jealous!" said Tamnâ, while her friend looks at the soldier curiously, like a child gazing at an irritated cockchafer. "You're jealous! Of whom? Of Taravant? Ah, *mon général,* this fellow has never kissed my fingertips—but not because he hasn't wanted to, of course. Try to understand, finally, that Taravant can give me roles, a thousand roles, all roles, and know that I, who drink Château-Margaux from a glass caressed by golden arabesques, who is adored and served on the knees like a queen, would lick the mud from the gutter for a good role, and clean the pavement with my tongue!"

LI
SMALL WORLD

In their icy hovel, the man and the woman are drunk and asleep, she on the ragged chair, he on the floor. The candle, about to go out, the red wick of which is carbonized and which is collapsing in cascades of tallow, only illuminates their lacerated and blood-stained faces with a ruddy glow—for they have fought, as usual, before collapsing, knocked out by eau-de-vie. Sitting on the edge of the bed devoid of sheets, almost naked, a poor three-year-old child is weeping with hunger and cold; but his big sister, who is six years old, picks him up, wraps him in her shawl, which has more holes than fabric, and, having nothing else to give him, calms his hunger and warms him up with kisses, and he falls asleep in her arms. And, magnified by celestial amour, the girl with the big golden eyes and the transparent flesh is already as beautiful and as serious as a young mother.

LII
FLOURISH!

She was called Nini when she was young and as beautiful as a goddess, and she is still called Nini now, when the furious fingernails of Old Age have hollowed out a thousand profound wrinkles in her tanned face and pulled out tufts of gray hair from beneath her headscarf, like the clumps of wool that one pulls out of a mattress. Nini's rags, her smock, her woolen coat and her skirt, no longer have either form or color. Everything is ripped, tied in hideous knots, and mended with bits of thread. The old woman has no stockings and the tops of her bare feet stick out of her masculine shoes like rude tongues.

However, in thinking about the past, Nini does not regret the garments, nor the house, nor the silk furniture, nor the sprightly carriages of her good times. The only thing to which she cannot resign herself is no longer having flowers—her, to whom the Prince of Messina once sent a basket of lilacs every morning, for her awakening!

Suddenly, she sees on the ground the debris of an old bouquet of roses that has been thrown away in the street, and with her bony fingers she picks up the stripped petals, seizing them, still stained with mud, and she sniffs them voluptuously.

LIII
CHAMBER MUSIC

It is the Sunday of the Grand Prix.[1] The golden sun has expelled the rain, suddenly swept away, and Paris, devoid of carriages, is as cheerful as a little provincial town. All alone in his miserable little room, old Esperat is perfectly certain that he does not even have a sou with which to buy a small loaf of bread, but that does not matter to him, because he has his violin—and, indeed, he is playing the violin.

To the sound of the crazy music a green forest appears, and Pierrot, who, sitting on the grass, is guzzling a snipe pâté and drinking rosé wine from a bottle. And gradually, still playing, Esperat senses that he has become Pierrot himself; he savors the delicate game and the bright chilled transparency, the color of topaz, aromatized with juniper. It is in vain that the bearded Arlequin with the cardboard face and Columbine, in a beret and a little mantle with golden buttons, pass back and forth behind him, drinking occasionally from his glass and stealing a few morsels; he has the best part nevertheless. But suddenly, *snap!* the chanterelle breaks. The old musician has no spare strings in his dwelling, that one is two short to be repaired, and Arlequin, Pierrot, Columbine, the pâté and the forest full of birds all disappear, vanishing into the gray dust of the room, under the sad snuff-box skylight.

"There we go," says Esperat resignedly, putting his dear violin back in its case. "I certainly shan't be dining today."

---

1 The Grand Prix de Paris, in which French three-year-old thoroughbreds race against international opposition, is run at Longchamp in July.

LIV
POETIC ART

The Academicians are in session. They are talking in low voices, expressing themselves in well-chosen words, and their serene faces express a complete bliss. They have to award a prize for poetry to the best work composed on a given subject: "The Influence of the *Revue des Deux Mondes* in the Far East," and on the proposal of the amiable novelist Tonia, whose well-combed side-whiskers are undulating like the waters of a silver stream, they are about to accord their unanimous suffrage to number eleven, which, with the most touching modesty, has adopted the epigraph *Sinite parvulos venire ad vos.*[1] But at that moment, a centenarian Academician rises to his feet, surging forth from the shadow. The hall is perfectly illuminated by its windows, but that shadow has been secreted around him by the old immortal. Dry and brown, he seems to have been sculpted in a box-tree root, and he is so old that hair is beginning to grow again after ages have passed, on his smooth cranium, as blond as that of a child. And as the delicate Tonia repeats, with a grace further refined by a hint of subtle irony:

"Yes, Messieurs. I dare to believe that you will choose number eleven, without asking yourselves too much whether this is not the sauce—I mean the epigraph—that can do

---

1 The quotation from the gospel, attributed to Jesus, ends *ad meum* [i.e., "suffer the little children to come to me"] rather than *ad vos* [to you].

without rhymes, and that you will, in favor of the intention, crown the poem…"

The little old man, waving his wooden hands furiously, howls :"It can't be crowned because within it, there's a *rejet!*"[1]

---

1 The several layers of this wordplay make its translation and appreciation difficult, even if one is aware of the massive chip that the author had on his shoulder in consequence of his own rejection by the Academy and his confirmed enmity to free verse. The several meanings of the word *rejet* include a new shoot put out by an old tree and a device employed in poetry by which one line runs into the next (as the phrases of the vignette have just done).

LV
GALLANT PROMENADE

As agile and undulating as a snake and as solemn as Fatality, delightfully made-up and rosy, molded expressly by her black satin dress with caressant gathers, which clutches her as if to choke her, with the patience and the proud resignation of a slave, a *fille de joie et de douleur*,[1] launching gazes that awaken desire like darts incessantly, relentlessly and untiringly, is meekly walking back and forth outside a pharmacist's shop, in which a green bottle and a red bottle are ablaze, illuminated by gas. Why does the *fille de joie*, in her eternal march, never get past the pharmacist's shop? The passers-by do not know; she does not know herself, and perhaps in restricting her errant course thus, that total exile, whose golden heels scarcely sound on the bitumen, is unconsciously obeying a symbolic necessity.

She goes slowly, which an expertly rhythmic and musical step, spreading around her the immense void of her thought

---

1 Again, this wordplay does not translate easily, a literal rendition as "daughter of joy and pain" being unable to take aboard the usual signification of *fille de joie*—i.e., prostitute, or streetwalker. Pairs of large bottles containing water dyed red and green were frequently employed emblematically by French pharmacists in their window-displays. Although electrically-controlled traffic lights had not yet made an appearance on the streets of Paris when the story first appeared, and would not do so until the 1920s, the two colors were already symbolically associated with "stop" and "go."

and the charm of her horrible grace. She goes past the green bottle and the red bottle by turns, which envelop her with her bright reflection, and as if she were already being caressed and kissed by the flames of Hell, the *fille de douleur et de joie* appears alternately to be red and green.

LVI
VISITING LADY

Sitting on a stool in front of a small white wood table on which an old skull as yellow as amber is placed, Brother Foulques is reading Origen's *Hexapia* in his bare cell. Paler than his white robe, the monk's face, although young, is labored by Meditation, which has hollowed out profound wrinkles on his forehead and cheeks, and his hairless cranium is as smooth as an ivory tablet. Meanwhile, without any key having been inserted into the lock, the door opens, turning silently on its hinges, and a She-Devil enters with a light and deliberate step. She is young, beautiful, svelte and as naked as a rock in the countryside or a pebble in a silver stream, and the light plays on the calm whiteness of her abdomen. A ray of sunlight creases the pink toenails of her parted feet and the rose-buds of her breasts, and she is coiffed with russet hair that is nothing but luminous vapor and is not yet flame-red.

She is naked, and she is wearing a necklace and earrings made of sapphires and black pearls. Politely, but without interrupting his reading, Foulques makes a sign that signifies: "Please sit down," and the She-Devil does indeed sit down on the second stool, which was empty. She knows that she does not have the right to speak to the monk unless he speaks to her or allows her to see a glimmer of desire in his eyes, but the minutes and the hours go by without the brother paying the slightest attention to his indiscreet visitor. It is in vain that she exhausts the entire arsenal of her coquetries. She flutters her eyelashes, she crosses and uncrosses her legs, she fans herself with a fan the color of moonlight; sometimes she seems to be about to faint, or, with a modest gesture, she hides her breasts with her transparent fingers; at other times she is as cheerful as a flock of birds and she shows her white teeth. But before all these provocations the studious monk does not stir any more than a block of wood. He reads tranquilly, and the little widow of his cell is reflected on his smooth cranium. Finally discouraged, the female demon decides to leave as she entered, and disappears, only leaving behind the vague perfume of her ruddy hair.

"As frivolous as a woman," mutters the monk Foulques, and, without thinking any longer about the She-Devil, he leans over the volume open before him and continues his assiduous reading.

LVII
ILE SAINT-LOUIS

On the quayside, near a willow whose enormous roots have emerged violently from the soil and crawled on to the pavement, the Angler is fishing, surrounded by his baskets and his rods, holding a big net in his hands, as motionless as if he were made of stone.

It is already evening; on the opposite bank, in the indecisive mist, a stiff, desolate being protruding from the ground like a black lily, braces himself and jumps, and the sinister green water closes over him silently. The Angler has seen the incident perfectly, but the muscles of his face have not stirred in consequence, nor has his rod trembled in his hand. What does it matter to him whether one mortal more or less is dragging the rude burden of this life and stringing together futile words like a necklace of fake pearls? The important thing, for him, is to know whether or not a gudgeon will bite. He is fishing; he is there, as always; he was there under the reign of Charles X and it is easy to divine that he will always be there.

He has seen republics and empires pass; he has heard festival songs of joy, the merry laughter of young women, the sound of fusillades and the galloping of heavy cavalry on the sonorous pavement. One day, he saw a great red and pink light in the sky, when Paris burned, but he did not seek to know what was burning. In our feverish epoch, when drama has prevailed through innumerable changes visibly executed by a mechanism similar to a broken clock, only the Angler has not modified his function or his attitude. He is fishing with a line, and in him is summarized henceforth the spirit of succession and invincible continuity of the French soul.

LVIII
SPAIN

In the ball given by Madame la Duchesse de Fernand-Nunez to inaugurate the drawing-rooms of her new house, while Her Majesty Queen Isabella makes her entrance on the arm of the Spanish Ambassador, and everyone is admiring in their rich costumes Madame Velasco, in pale pink, Madame la Marquise de San Carlos, with a diadem on her head, Mesdames Penalver, de Cartagena and d'Umbaren, and a hundred other beauties and cavaliers covered in medals, the poet never wearies of considering two men who, by virtue of their aspect of strange and gripping originality, cut through all the rest.

One, who resembles the late and lamented caricaturist Cham,[1] and the tips of whose moustache are turned up, as furious and as thin as swords, while reckless bravery shines in his soft and benevolent eyes, is as thin as a rake. The other, almost still a child, pale under his long black hair, as strong as a lion and as handsome as a god, has a gaze charged with amour and desire, traversed by flashes, burning with an irresistible flame, and his lips, scarcely caressed by a light down, are like crimson flowers. As they pass by, all the women—princesses, duchesses and young women with ingenuous faces—tremble like roses in a storm wind, or madly-palpitating birds in an electric cloud. The poet follows the two men in question with a curious and delighted eye, but does not even think of informing himself as

---

1 "Cham" was the signature attached to his illustrations by Charles-Amédée de Noé (1818-1879), primarily associated with *Le Charivari*.

to their names; for those names might have been changed by family events or the caprice of kings; but how could he, a poet, fail to recognize in those two heroic figures a descendant of the knight Don Quixote and the youngest son, adored himself, of the adored Don Juan Tenorio?

LIX
INTRIGUED WOMAN

In the middle of the Opéra ball, where thick and lazy luminous dust is already floating, is that a young man reposing there on a bench in the foyer or a woman in a masculine costume? In any case, no more beautiful and more perfect creature has ever been modeled in living clay. Under the tapering hat with a broad and turned-up rim, thick and short dark golden hair is accumulated; the features charm simultaneously with the most feminine grace and the most virile energy. The pure eyebrows are infinitely silky, and above the crimson mouth, like a ripe fruit, an impalpable blond down is visible.

On the bare neck, which a turned-down collar surrounds without hiding it, there is no trace of the ignoble infirmity known as an Adam's apple, and yet, in spite of the emphatic hips, the firm and agile body is surely that of a boy; must it not veritably be that of a young cavalier, and not a disguised young woman, in order to wear that black suit correctly? But although certainly vigorous, those long hands, delicately gloved, are evidently a woman's, and those are also a woman's feet. In sum, there is throughout the allure of the individual something definite and masculine, which ends up troubling those who look at it.

The tall Cora was bored enough to swallow her tongue, but she is no longer bored since she has seen that beautiful mysterious being. She is sitting next to him, speaking to him tenderly, madly, wittily, tearful with emotion; she is telling her chaplet, but, unfurling the scales of a rich and melodious voice, the bizarre child responds in curt phrases in which all the inflexions of indifference succeed one another, as insensible to words as a merchant of speech, and to sentiments as an old courtesan.

"Well," says the tall Cora in a strangled voice, who no longer knows what the devil to say and who is at the end of her tether, "decidedly, are you a man or a woman?"

"My dear," the seated infant says, "you're very curious. I'm not sure myself."

LX
FIRST AMOURS

Illuminated by their lanterns, hooked on to nails pink with rust, the four rag-pickers—the thin Lefoi, Madame Loeil with the tragic face, Mère Bobilier and Biribi, as old as the world—are squatting on the floor in a dirty room, black and leprous, in which wallpaper detached by the damp is floating in streamers; and cheerfully, they are savoring a vague feast, more frightful than that of Thyestes, for the elements of it have been picked out of the rubbish at street corners. In the shadow, against the wall, bundles, sacks and hooks are leaning curiously; and, buoyed up by the bottle of gut-rot that is circulating, which they are drinking in gulps, the good friends start laughing, each of the four showing five or six teeth; they are chatting playfully about what pleases ladies, and, from thread to needle, have just agreed that each of them will recount her first adventure and how the whim came to her.

Mére Lefoi, who has had misfortunes since, was the daughter of a grocer. It was a friend of the family, a decorated employee to whom her parents confided her, who, holding her by the hand, took her for a walk in the quarries, and there, taking out a pistol, threatened to kill her if she did not listen to his madrigals.

At exactly fifteen years of age, Madame Loeil had been married to a zinc-worker; on the wedding night he was as drunk as thirty-six thousand men, and he took hold of her by the hair in order to tell her how pretty she was.

At the age of twelve Mère Bobillier had looked so often through keyholes and learned about life so well that in consequence of those studies she had hidden in a dog-kennel with her friend Zidore, a kid as wily as a monkey, to play husband and wife.

Then comes the turn of old Biribi, whose skirt, which she has tucked up, allows the sight of boots. But no matter how hard she tries, she cannot remember; she makes an enormous effort, extending her stupid mouth desperately, and finally, plunging her two closed fists into her bald cranium, over which a tuft of hair is projected, she says:

"I don't know any longer. I think it was the relatives."

SIXTH DOZEN

LXI
THE GODDESS

In a broad clearing, under the moon's rays, the great Artemis, sated with carnage, is sitting with her warrior huntresses. She sees opposite her a mound, which advances like a peninsula into the sea, where two silver stream resembling eyes are staring at her brazenly. Immediately, the goddess frowns, and on the hill an enormous black foliage springs forth and grows, which hides the vague indiscreet eyes.

Happy then, content with herself, proud of her victory and of her horrible virginity, she passes her beautiful hands over the dead hinds lying beside her in the grass, which the wounds of her prey leave bloody, while her dogs lick up the pools of blood voluptuously.

But then a furious noise of horns resounds and, shivering with terror, Artemis feels herself lacerated all the way to the entrails, sees a black mass pass though the trees, carried away at a hectic run, and hears the packs of the frightful hunter Amour howling in the night.

LXII
LITTLE WOMEN

In the Avenue Trudaine, in a deepening dusk, three little girls are walking hand in hand: three terrible little girls, already as vicious as women. They are strutting boldly and darting provocative glances around them.

All three are dressed in bizarre rags, but carefully selected. Phrasie has a pink ribbon around her neck; Tapon is wearing a hat, to which she has attached a feather that she has picked up at a street-corner, and Coqueluche has stuffed her little hands into long suede gloves. A clean-shaven old man, decorated, with a furtive step approaches them, speaks to them in a low voice, and they start to laugh proudly, thinking that they are true demoiselles, but the old rag-picker Simone, black, wrinkled and centenarian, passes by with her package on her back—because she is too poor to have a basket—her long white hair flying in the wind. She raises her hook to the sky indignantly and, looking the monsieur full in the face, howls into the gathering darkness like a she-wolf, in a tragic voice:

"Rags for sale!"

LXIII
SUMMER PLEASURES

Baronne Edmée has been planning her coup for a long time, choosing the hour when she will extend her nets. She knows that her most intimate enemy, Marquise Thaïs, has a big pedestal, like the Venus de Milo and Queen Berthe, and she savors in advance the joy of humiliating her in front of Comtesse Hermine and Comtesse Jeanne. At Étretat, on a summer afternoon when the sun is tinting the struts of the lowered Venetian blinds gold, in Comtesse Hermine's chalet, from which the song of the sea can be heard, the four women are sprawling on the silk divans in the pink boudoir, and with an infernal cunning, Edmée steers the conversation toward the pretty eighteenth-century gouaches in which rosy Eglés are comparing the whiteness of their breasts and the slenderness of their legs, Finally, she talks about comparing their feet, throws off her slippers, and shows off, in pale blue stockings, the prettiest little feet imaginable.

After her, Hermine and Jeanne also show their silk-clad feet, which have nothing vulgar about them, and the moment finally arrives when Marquise Thaïs is about to suffer a cruel anguish! But Thaïs is untroubled, for she knows everything that the pretty Edmée is carrying in her head, and how the coiffeur accumulates thereon brown curls bought from a merchant of Ladies' Hair. And as, with an imperious gaze, Edmée seems to be saying to her: "Your turn now!" she says, with a calm pride: "No, I don't show my feet. This is what I show!"

And, detaching her comb, she shows, liberates and causes to flow down her back an avalanche of heavy, thick and fine blonde hair, full of ecstatic flames and transparent shadows. And as there is a pile of gold for donation to the poor on a red lacquer table, she picks up a gold coin and, as if it were lead, bends it in two with her strong teeth and adds, triumphantly: "And that too!"

Baronne Edmée is no longer laughing. She brings her little feet back under her dress, shamefully, looks at her enemy with a penitent expression in her green eyes, and thinks privately how pleasant it would be to be able to slice that soft flesh thinly.

LXIV
THE NOTARY'S WIFE

Taking advantage of the feast day, the notary, Monsieur Pin, has gone fishing, and as there are no thieves in the pretty little town of Nioul, when the maidservant went shopping she has left the door of the house ajar—with the consequence that, arriving with his father's letter, young Saturnin Lorion, scarcely sixteen years old, decides to go in, to climb the old staircase, and to go on at hazard, straight to the bedroom of Madame Rosine Pin.

The window overlooking the garden is open; the weather is summery, warm and delightful. Through the lowered Venetian blinds, on which the sun is designing golden flowers, a thousand perfumes and a thousand murmurs rise. Feeling amorous, while the notary, her husband, is out fishing, the disheveled young woman, scarcely veiled by a transparent chemise from which the pink nipples of her breasts protrude, is sprawling on a divan, one leg here and one there, and a ray of sunlight is caressing her charming feet. Having entered that scene, young Saturnin Lorion does not know what to do, loses his head, and, throwing himself upon Madame Pin like Poverty upon the world, kisses her hands, her arms her eyes, her hair and everything! Enlaced by two snowy arms, he loses all notion of right and wrong and rolls recklessly through abysms of felicity; but when the pretty lady collects herself, he experiences a need, by virtue of a scruple, to justify himself.

"Madame," he says, "I've brought a letter from my father to Monsieur your husband. I'm his petty clerk."

"Not so petty," says the notary's wife, licking her lips.

LXV
ROSES AND LILIES

In the garden of the brilliant poet, flowering at the same time, are a large bunch of Roses and a large bunch of Lilies. The Lilies and the Roses are intoxicated by joy. The mild summer breeze is caressing them and the sunlight is kissing them, and the bright petals of their corollas rise up like fiery gems. In a voice that makes no sound but is nevertheless audible, the mysterious voice that emerges from things thought to be inanimate, they say, while bathing in the light:

"We Flowers are fortunate, because we live in the garden of the honest poet, where we accomplish the function appropriate to us, and where we exist purely and simply as Flowers, without fear of furnishing a pretext for classical tropes and being employed as a term of comparison. And as no philistine will come into this garden, and no spouter of commonplaces, no one will claim that we have any relationship with the winged butterflies, which is as stupid as supposing amours between doves and crocodiles. And we, the Lilies with straight petals and green buds, will lift up our golden pistils gloriously, and we, the blushing Roses with ecstatic hearts, will flourish for no reason, for pleasure, as Caussade killed Latournelle,[1] without being constrained to affirm the pretended whiteness of red or green women, and without submitting to the humiliation of being compared to any demoiselle."

---

1 Reportedly, in Victor Hugo's play about a notorious courtesan, *Marion de Lorme* (1826).

LXVI
THE PRETTY COUPLE

In the Café des Officiers at Saint-Meuris, Mademoiselle Zéphirine descends to the counter, white, sentimental, like a holy missal, coiffed in the bangs of a pretty woman, squeezed into her tight dress, and sits down between two vases of flowers in an irreproachable keepsake pose.[1] It is not a secret from anyone that Mademoiselle Zéphirine is madly smitten with Lieutenant Adhémar de Saint-Saigne, the prettiest and slimmest of all known hussars, Rightly or wrongly, but doubtless rightly, she imagines that the ravishing young man with the soft girlish face will not pay any attention to her as long as she does not succeed is becoming as slender as him. She is thin; she is a bee, but Adhémar is a wasp. On seeing her appear, the stout Major Ledurubey has not been able to retain a cry of admiration.

"*Come et massacre!*"[2] he says. "Zéphirine is even better corseted than yesterday. She'll get there, *mille trompettes!*"

"Or she'll die," says Captain Louiseau, philosophically, placing the double-six.

---

1 The committee of the Académie Française charged with maintaining the purity of the French language did not permit the term "keepsake," borrowed from English, to exist in correct French, but Banville, in spite of his reputation for poetic severity, was not so strict when writing comedy and this is not the only occasion in *La Lanterne magique* where he employs it.
2 "Come" also exists in Franglais, but the speaker is presumably employing a different argot, in which the term applies to an officer in a correctional prison camp.

Finally, Adhemar comes in; he directs happy glances around him, gives a few handshakes here and there, orders his absinthe and turns up the tips of his moustache, but pays no more heed to Zéphirine than if she were a hundred thousand feet underground. Then Adhémar goes to the mirror and admires himself delightedly. Strictly molded in his blue dolman, he is a thousand times slimmer than the demoiselle at the counter. He could hold a little girl in his ten fingers and pass through a ring. He contemplates himself and finds himself adorable, and yet, out of human respect, he does not blow kisses to his image reflected by the obliging mirror. Desperately, Zéphirine goes back up to her room, breaks twenty laces, and finally succeeds in diminishing by a centimeter. But when she has come down again, she understands, by measuring the lieutenant's slender waist with her eye, how far she is from being able to compete with him. And as Joseph, the waiter, comes to ask her whether she would like him to serve her breakfast, the slender demoiselle raises her amorous eyes languidly and gazes at Adhémar as the expelled Eve must have gazed at the gates of the terrestrial paradise.

"No," she says, "just give me a small glass of vinegar."

LXVII
THE HEDGE RACE

With an inexplicable disdain for bulls, the truculent colorist Zardo is hunting in the plain of Marlotte clad in his scarlet coat, and he is shooting hares instead of painting landscapes, which is delaying and adjourning proportionately his entry to the Institut. The gamekeeper Juguelet passes by, twisted and withered by the years, but still obstinate in his duty and as brave as a lion in spite of his catarrh. He sees the artist, and as that giant in a Rubens hat with a flowing beard, whose legs are protected by violet greaves, does not give him the impression of a man who must be in regulation, he marches straight up to him and asks him point blank for his hunting permit.

But at the moment when Zardo opens his mouth, he takes off like an eagle, like a dart or a whistling arrow. Juguelet launches himself after him, but too late; the painter is already far away. He is running like Milanion[1] pursued by Atalanta and throwing his golden apples; he devours, swallows and suppresses distance. Juguelet, coughing, panting and sweating, follows him despairingly, madly, with the anguish of the futile contest, but he follows him! Like two horses in a steeplechase,

---

1 In a story recycled by several Greek and Roman authors, Milanion, or Melanion, is an alternative name for Hippomenes, who wanted to marry the reluctant huntress Atalanta, who had been told by an oracle that any suitor would have to beat her in a foot race or be struck dead; Aphrodite helped him to win by suggesting that he distract the huntress by dropping golden apples that she gave him. The race was duly won, but the couple were subsequently turned into lions by Cybele.

they leap hedges, rocks and streams, everything that opposes their passage; they traverse woods in which it is cold and steppes in which one roasts. Zardo encounters a horse and, passing over the beast's back, jumps over it, making the perilous leap. Juguelet passes under the animal's belly, and they go on thus, carried away, launched at full speed, lifted up by an invisible hurricane. Sometimes, Juguelet thinks that he is about to catch up with Zardo, but immediately sees him two hundred meters in front of him. Finally, he reaches him, and, in a hoarse, strangled, frightful voice, more dead than alive, howls and sighs three words: "Your gun permit!"

The artist has stopped dead. He takes the piece of paper demanded from his pocket and offers it to his interlocutor with the most exquisite politeness.

"But in that case," says the nonplussed gamekeeper, whose breast resembles a broken bellows, "why, when you saw me, did you start running?"

"Monsieur," says the artist, coldly, "that assertion is not exact. On the one hand, I saw you, and on the other, I started running, because I love to run; but there was no connection between the two phenomena in question!"

LXVIII
LITERARY CRITCISM

Clad in a silk chemise embroidered with capricious designs, Josèphe Osli, sunk in a low armchair covered in Venetian needlepoint is reading the latest novel. On the floor, in front of the creole whom the Parisian nobility is courting, her favorite maidservant Lyzie, a beautiful colored girl, as yellow as amber, whose heavy hair disperses a black sheet around her head, is lying naked. Josèphe places her feet, clad in pink stockings, on that living carpet, and, while smoking a cigarette of Indian tobacco, drinks small sips of a peppery beverage composed by her old negress Hébé, who is as savant as Locusta. When she has replaced her glass on the ivory side-table, she resumes reading her book, sometimes very quietly and sometimes in a loud voice. It is the terrible new novel, the terrifying and sadistic volume that has recently appeared, which is making the frightened Naturalists tremble, and in which an audacious seeker, who does not recoil before anything, has believed that he is depicting the soul of courtesans.

"Well," says Josèphe, disdainfully, closing the book, "authors are decidedly innocent!"

"To make one weep!" murmurs Lyzie, in a slow and musical voice.

"Yes," says Josèphe. "Their brains are decorated interiority with white silk. But what would become of those poor ingenuous souls if they could glimpse what we were thinking for a single minute? Wouldn't they be deaf and mute with astonishment, and then changed into seven-legged calves and sky blue crocodiles?"

LXIX
THE HIDING PLACE

"No, Agénor, my dear little husband, you'll never know the extent to which I'm faithful!" says the pretty Madame Léontine Astiés, whose brown hair, scattered over the pillow, tickles the nose of the tax-collector while those sweet words tickle his heart. "For me," adds the amiable joker with the turned-up nose, "any man who isn't you has the effect on me of a toad, Can you understand, then, how one might love a lancer, as so many women in the city do? Oh, if a lancer were only to kiss the tip of my glove, even when I had snatched it away, I'd rather be cut into little pieces!"

Her forehead and her hair having been kissed a thousand times for that fine speech, Léontine gets up and puts on a peignoir, while Agénor never wearies of repeating: "Oh, what good luck to have such a faithful wife!" Soon, however, that exclamation is no longer sufficient for him, he stands up on the bed, and in his ecstasy, bounding and leaping in time, he begins to sing, to the tune of *Lampions*: "So faithful! So faithful! So faithful!" Then the violence of his choreography detaches the awning of the bed, of which only the platform remained, the curtains having been recently removed, and in a cloud of dust, with the awning that served them as a hiding place, like a flock of butterflies and crazy birds, or a white swirl of furious snow, the love-letters that Madame Léontine has been piling up there for a long time, and is still amassing in dozens, fall, flutter and

166

accumulate in hundreds and thousands, with knotted bunches of various favors.

Astiés opens one, ten, twenty of them: they are all letters from lancers, which call his wife "my little puss," "my little bunny" or "my little mouse." She has loved lancers, a great many lancers, all lancers! On the forehead and face of the tax-collector, the pale lilies of death blossom. He falls unconscious, as if his heart has been traversed by the lances of all those lancers who designate his wife by the names of animals; for, as he comprehends in a last flash of thought, it is to infidelity alone that she is faithful.

LXX
MEN OF THE WORLD

Laced up as tightly as a Vire eel in its rigid coat, the handsome, elegant and divine concierge Monsieur Rodolphe Capitain, sprawling in a plush armchair embroidered with silk flowers, is caressing his fine blond beard with his pale fingers and smoking an equally blond cigarette, like a *Belle aux cheveux d'or*.[1] Everything respires the luxury, joy and tranquility of triumph in the lodge hung with red Oriental cloth with yellow designs, where a scullion in snow-white garments is cooking the traditional *miroton* in a silver saucepan.

While Monsieur Capitan surrounds himself with spirals of blue smoke, his wife Jane—with an A because it is more English—having just closed the *Revue des Deux Mondes*, is working on garments for poor children, and on the grand piano painted with little rises on a bright green background, his swan-necked daughter Ada is playing a *Reverie* by Chopin, raising her desolate blue eyes. Meanwhile, the functionary nonchalantly removes the rubber band from the *Journal officiel* and scans the list of distinctions awarded in accordance with the national fête. Then, throwing his unextinguished cigar into the lapis lazuli spittoon, he says:

"Well, this year is just the same as all the others! I see that they haven't yet decorated a single concierge!"

---

1 The title of a well-known story by Madame d'Aulnoy, and also the soubriquet by which the English nursery-tale character Goldilocks is known in France.

LXXI
THE INTERROGATION

In the immense drawing-room of the Pierre-Fort town house in the Rue de Babylone, as vast as a desert, in which the heroic tapestries, the mantled fireplaces, the sculpted gold candlesticks, the furniture clad in antique damask and the portraits of captains in armor and white cravats and austere ladies costumed as Diana with sashes of flowers evoke vanished times, all the males of the family are gathered in tribunal and are judging an accused.

The accused is a young Auvergnat from Joze, the water-carrier Chevenon, ingenuous, as robust as Hercules, coiffed by a thick shock of black hair, whose nascent beard scarcely shades his pink and healthy face. Here are the facts: Mademoiselle Yolande de Pierre-Fort, as beautiful as a lily in the splendid grace of her sixteen years, has been seduced; she is pregnant, and it has been discovered that the guilty party is none other than the Auvergnant Chevenon. Evidently, the wretch is only the instrument of an intrigue cleverly woven by audacious speculators dreaming of appropriating the twenty million that the rich heiress will one day bring together over her head.

It is a matter of confessing him, of making him tell everything, of seizing via his admissions the thread of the conspiracy. In order better to intimidate and disturb the young rascal, the Piere-Forts have put on their rosettes, their medals and their juridical, sacerdotal and military uniforms, and they are all attacking him with their particular resources and their professional intelligence. Vidame Guy is peppering him with fine epigrams; Archbishop Mainfroi is speaking to him unctuously; General Roland is threatening him in a thunderous voice; and, as the white-haired Président Yves, magnificent in his ermine and scarlet robe, presses him once again to reveal what complicated motive he was obeying, Chevenon, blushing all the way to the eyes and wringing his cap in his hands, responds to the illustrious magistrate:

"Damn it, mochieu, I'll tell you. The demoigelle asked me, and then, I was sgared of losing my job!"

LXII
THE TOILETTE

It is Saturday night, already past midnight. Since the morning, the Devil's mother has been working like a slave, because today she has been very busy with the housework. She has finished ironing and folding her linen, and has arranged it in good order in the big cupboards. She has scoured her skewers with sand, her decorated yellow copper saucepans with pumice-stone, her wrought iron saucepans with Spanish bleach and then she has washed the floor-tiles of the hall with detergent, which she has wiped off subsequently with a big sponge. Now, she is occupied with her son, the Devil, who, although he is very old, still gives her the impression of a child.

She has made him sit down on a little stool and she is combing his red hair with a coral comb. Usually the Devil submits to that operation with the most intimate sensuality, but this time, on the contrary, he is agitated by shudders, and long sobs are escaping his convulsed breast. The old lady knows full well why; it is because her son is smitten lately with a thin green she-devil who is inflicting all possible miseries on him.

"So, my poor boy," she says, "has that cruel Tara given you another tangled thread to unwind?"

"Oh, Maman," sighs the Devil, and on hearing that sweet word caress her old heart, the lady senses something like a drop of water in the corner of her eye, which she is about to shed. She does not let it drop, because those folk never weep, but in the end, for the thousandth part of a second, she has the panic, the thrill, the hope and the delectable illusion of a tear.

SEVENTH DOZEN

LXXIII
A BAD BUSINESS

As if Prudhon[1] had clothed her, with her tight dress and her Greek caloquet, the merchant of Amours, holding her cage in her hand, is going along the Rue d'Aumale, where the gracious Aurélie Flament is taking the air, sitting in her ground-floor window.

"My beautiful demoiselle," says the merchant, "buy one or two of my Amours! They're very nice, happy, faithful, as gentle as a newborn lamb, and I'll let you have them cheap."

The cheerful young woman looks at the cage and all the winged children fluttering over the frail perches. She admires all their innocent eyes, their hair like a golden fog, their pretty little poses, their plump bodies and limbs, their financiers' midriffs, their rosy buttocks and all their fresh and becoming flesh, dotted by a thousand dimples.

"My word!" she says, giving a substantial handful of gold to the merchant, who goes away charmed, with a sly expression, "I'll buy the cage and all the Amours."

She is delighted to see the ingenuous little beings; but they are immediately transfigured, and start to take on rascally and violent appearances. Wild and menacing, their eyes hidden by their bushy hair, which has turned black, they are showing themselves as they really are, cruel and thirsty for carnage. One

---

1 The painter Pierre-Paul Prud'hom (1758-1823) was famous for his allegorical paintings, admired by Baudelaire, as well as his portraits of notable figures of the post-Revolutionary era.

is holding a cup of poison, another a bloody knife, and another a smoking torch. One, with side-whiskers, is coiffed with a top hat, as on the Boulevard de Batignolles, and they are singing songs in an argot that would make an African turco flinch.

Horrified, Aurélie turns her eyes away from that gang of murderers. But to console herself she has taken from the cage a very tint Amour, only just born, whose eyes are sky-blue and who still has a drop of milk on his rosy lips. She has posed him on her finger like a pet bird, and she says to him, while caressing him with her lily-white hand:

"Come and kiss mistress, chéri!"

But the little Amour has immediately stood up on the finger that bears him. He strikes a pose, his fist on his hip, and lights a cigar as thick as the point of a needle between his lips. Looking the beautiful young woman full in the face, he says to her, in a roguish little voice, as thin as that of a watch-spring:

"First, you know, Aurélie it's necessary not to put on airs!"

LXXIV
COUNSEL

In the month of June, while roses are flowering elsewhere, behind a cabaret situated in a little street that intersects the Rue de la Gaité in Montmartre, undertakers are at table in the garden; and it really is a garden appropriate to them, for nothing living grows there. The "arbors" there are uniquely composed of rotten planks, and against the black and oozing wall an equally rotten trellis is applied, on which nothing is suspended except for spiders' webs. On the ground, beaten and caved-in in places, broken flower-pots and the cadavers of watering-cans are strewn—but could they ever have done any watering in the time when they existed?

The waitress Eulalie, who has the confidence of the master of the house and who, pale, decrepit and terrible, seems to have emerged from a tomb, serves her guests whatever she wants, and as she wants. While emptying the violet mugs and battling against nutriments as indestructible as bronze, the black-clad fellows are chatting about women and reciting playful stories, but without professional seriousness departing from their faces for an instant.

Alongside them, an actor is sitting, so poor that he cannot present himself in the establishment where his comrades eat, and he is clad—in 1882!—in a green polonaise that no longer has any olives, but had them once. With the intrepidity of despair, Florigny is struggling against a rabbit-head that is laughing long because it is laughing last, and while he is attacking it, a great funereal yellow dog, lurking under the table, is attacking his calves and biting them. Annoyed, in the end, the actor kicks the dog, but a glance from his neighbor, the wise undertaker Pastre, immediately makes him understand the imprudence of his conduct.

In fact, the functionary indicates by a rapid gesture the fear that the omnipotent harridan ought to inspire in any customer concerned for his interests, and, doubtless expressing by means of a gripping and very Parisian hyperbole the intense amity with which old women attach themselves to their animals, he murmurs very quietly in his ear:

"If you want Eulalie to treat you amiably, it's necessary not to harm the dog. He's her lover."

LXXV
THE SYBARITE

The adorable Isidore Nieul is lying voluptuously between her sheets of Flanders cloth, which, almost as soft as her flesh, are enveloping and caressing her. Half-awake and half-asleep, by the soft lamplight burning in a crystal chandelier, she gazes at the birds fluttering in the great forest of flowers in the pale lilac silk that lines her bedroom walls, and the fish with golden scales swimming in the silver steam. She savors the immense joy of reigning, of being beautiful, loved and faithfully served, of being naked in the fresh and perfumed bed, adrift in her long tawny hair, scattered around her.

But in the midst of that profound peace, something has bruised and wounded her! Isidore utters howls; her maidservant Jocette comes running, and finds her in tears. The agile chambermaid examines the damage. It is the courtesan's thigh, the thigh of the goddess, that has been cruelly offended; indeed, the spot is quite pink. And here is the culprit: a piece of cigarette-paper, which having accidentally fallen into the bed, has brushed the flesh of snow and lilies and ravaged it thus. The worthy Josette, so funny with her mad eyes and her canine nose, is desolate; she soothes Madame and lavishes *alas*es, Suddenly, however, and without transition the beautiful Isidore stops crying and starts laughing as if to unhinge her jaws.

"Oh!" says Josette, whom nothing astonishes and who has also started to laugh. "What is Madame thinking?"

"My girl," says the injured woman, "I'm thinking about the time when I was sitting on a boundary marker, devouring avidly—with beautiful teeth, as you can see—a hunk of bread picked up from the rubbish, in the days when my feet were shod in a hole around which a tiny bit of shoe remained: an old shoe thrown into the gutter by an invalid—and when I combed my red hair with a nail!"

LXXVI
HYPERBOLES

On the little village square where night has already fallen, in a ground-floor room whose door is wide open, old Nanette Migne is finishing sewing a calico skirt by the light of her little lamp; and sitting a short distance away from her at a round walnut table, the young notary Monsieur Oscar Fourneri, an elegant fellow, is drinking a bottle of beer. Nanette Migne is a dressmaker by profession, but she has a barrel of beer in her cellar; on Sundays only she sells beer to a few peasants, and that is why she has had a sign placed over her door, on which the wheelwright, who is also the glazier, has done his best to paint the word CAFÉ.

Monsieur Fourneri, who lives directly opposite the dressmaker, has beer exactly like Nanette's, bought from the same merchant, but as he has been a student in Paris, and he misses all his excursions to the brasseries of the Latin Quarter, he comes to drink at Nanette's because of the word CAFÉ written above the door.

Meanwhile, the devoted Madame Euphrasie Fourneri is in despair. As tragic and disheveled as Lady Macbeth, she wrings her hands dolorously and cries with a somber anguish:

"O Heaven, how unhappy I am! My husband is at the café! He can't unaccustom himself to the café. *He leads the Café life!*"

And, soaking her insufficient handkerchief once again in the flood of her tears, she asks herself silently what she ought to do if the Senate, weary of always saying no, decides to vote for the Divorce Law.

LXXVII
THE NAÏVE GIRL

Père Andoche, a Capuchin friar who has come to Vannes to preach during Lent, is a saint as ugly as a devil. His aged face seems to have been carved with a hatchet in some gnarled tree trunk, and his scratchy beard is like a rare plant that sheep have already grazed. But as he knows marvelously how to conduct his flock where he wishes, sometimes by the caress of a persuasive voice and at other times with good thrusts of the crook, fecund in resources for curing souls, he is never at a loss. Penitents abound at his confessional in the old church whose perforated belfry launches forth into the open sky.

He has already expedited beautiful ladies and peasant women, whom he has sent away as neat and white as the laundry drying in the green meadow after bleaching, when the pretty Guillemette Josselin kneels before him, whose breast is raised by profound sobs and who, beneath her embroideries and her golden hat, is weeping like a young Magdalen. That is because she has seen the son of the seigneur passing through the gorse, young Comte Olivier, mounted on his Syrian horse, and, seeing him so handsome, has had the desire to kiss him. Now she believes herself to be damned irredeemably, and she is striking and bruising her breast with all her childish strength. Père Andoche does not hide from Guillemette that it is a serious matter; nevertheless, he does not want the death of the sinner, and after having ordered her to recite many orisons and paternosters, he adds:

"And as your sin has been that of wanting to kiss a handsome young man, for your penance you will kiss the ugliest and most displeasing man to be found in the parish."

"That will be you, then, *mon Père*," says the girl, slightly reassured, but who is blushing deeply, as if she could already feel on her rosy cheek the rude beard of the Capuchin.

LXXVIII
THE BLUE BOUTIQUE

Attracted, doubtless unconsciously, by the color of the sky, the celebrated mathematician and astronomer Jacques Nisolle, has come into a blue-painted barber's shop in the Rue Vaugirard in order to have himself shaved. When he is sitting down like a criminal and imprisoned in a napkin, after having been masked by soapy foam, and the scraping of his yellow skin begins, the scientist pursues his transcendent problems and continues his profound calculations, pushing the Xs of his algebra all the way to the azure of the Empyrean and the golden caverns where the gods are asleep.

At a certain moment, however, it seems to him that something like a great bird is fluttering around him and chilling him with the wind of its wings. He lifts his great head and looks. It is not a bird; it is the barber, in person, who is fluttering, absolutely in flight, whipping his hair with the air. He is launching himself, bounding and leaping like a clown, armed with his open razor, and all those capers he executes around the head of the scientist. Old Nisolle understands that if he moves, if he makes a gesture, his nose and his lips, menaced by the terrible razor, will be scythed like poppies in ripe wheat. Without emerging from his immobility, he raises his eyes with enormous lashes toward the lady sitting at the counter.

She is a keepsake beauty, an elegant and sentimental barber's wife, who rolls her gazelle eyes and makes a heart with her mouth. She sees the mathematician's legitimate curiosity and, pointing at her husband with an amiable and graciously sweeping gesture, she says:

"Don't pay any attention; it's just that he's mad."

And the madman resumes leaping, fluttering and launching himself as if on a trampoline. He is a southern madman, with a blue face and phosphoric eyes, Sometimes, he rises up like an aerostat, his black hair touching the ceiling, and then he comes down again, his razor still executing a formidable whirlwind of trenchant lightning around the petrified head. But without transition, he calms down, and, leaning toward the old man with such ardor that this time, his black hair sweeps the floor, he says:

"If you're content, you'll come back."

But Nisolle does not hear him. He puts a silver coin on the counter and goes out without waiting for his change. He has already forgotten that scene of massacre and has plunged his profound eyes back into infinity, amid the vertiginous Numbers and the swarming host of the Stars.

LXXIX
LOVE SCENE

The beautiful and gigantic Pauline Roche, a cantratrice built with Cyclopean stones, is sitting on a carpet with a white background at the feet of Gabriel Artas, and her vast blazing, overflowing golden blonde hair, untied, inundates her lover's knees. Right away, Gabriel wants to caress his beautiful mistress and talk amorously to her, charming her with praise, but Pauline stops him with a suppliant and imperious gesture.

"No," she says to him, "don't embrace me, don't kiss my trembling hands. Let me lie at your feet, immobile, silent, tamed, like a faithful bitch, savoring the annihilation of my will, intoxicating myself merely by thinking that I belong to you and that I'm your thing!"

The young man, who is no contrarian, lets his lover do as she wishes, but as he is not romantic either, having seen within arm's reach on a little chest of drawers with big feet a volume of Alexandre's Dumas' *Mousquetaires*, he opens it and, propping it up on other books, he amuses himself reading the adventures of d'Artagnan while his huge lover exhausts the mysterious joys of non-being. He does not weary of following the indefatigable Gascon and his friends, Athos, Porthos and Aramis, over hills and vales, but nevertheless, after a long moment, astonished by Pauline's amazing tranquility, he leans his head over her, and then sees that with her agile fingers, the enamored woman is diligently manipulating long needles, and, with a marvelous dexterity, knitting woolen socks.

LXXX
A LITTLE HISTORY

It is September 1982; in the pretty amphitheater constructed in the middle of the plain of Fontainebleau—where, it is said, there was once a verdant forest—thanks to the ingenious apparatus recently invented for amplifying the human voice without limit, a million spectators can easily hear the amiable lecturer Edgard Mour, so dear to the ladies. Under the gaze of the sympathetic professor, skulls are undulating like a sea of black waves, all similar and equally bushy since a means has been found of sowing and making hair grow like grass.

Uniformly clad in garments tailored in chemically-composed cloth, all those Parisian auditors appear to be the same age, thanks to tablet with the aid of which wrinkles can now be effaced, as the marks of pencils were once effaced with the aid of elastic gum. Being able thus to model themselves in accordance with their whim, the men appear in the splendor of their strength, but as for the women, none of them has consented to be more than sixteen years old, and under the sidereal illumination of the ethereal light, their dresses of thirty-two colors, embroidered with forty different metals, can be seen fluttering flamboyantly. Meanwhile the words of the charming Edgard Mour are imbibed; everyone is listening to them passionately, and the silence is so profound that in that seduced assembly, a deaf ear would hear a floating grain of dust.

"Yes, Mesdames et Messieurs," says the rosy-faced lecturer, "I do not hesitate to affirm, contrary to the doctrine of my honorable colleague Quinette, of the Academy of Facts and Documents, that the word *war*, which we discover so often in poems wrongly considered for a long time to be histories, only has an ideal and symbolic meaning and expresses, purely and simply, the contest of ideas. Can you believe, in fact, that really and literally, two troops of men, armed with murderous engines like those we employ in hunting, placed themselves facing one another with a mission to kill one another? I do not want, Messieurs, to abuse the advantage that reliable information gives me, and to criticize my beloved colleague without generosity, but is it not evident that, leaving aside those who led them, those flocks consecrated to death would have chosen that, each for his own part, meekly? If so, it would be necessary to admit that they preferred something else—but what?—to their own preservation. Or that in their own thought, everything would not finish for them with life—a hypothesis that, even presented conditionally, appears absurd."

LXXXI
AFTER THE PARTY

Having obtained his weekly allowance, Robert Vic, a robust Norman student with blond hair, has gone to dine alone at the Café Anglais, where, after having washed down his copious dinner with five or six bottles of fine wine, he had drunk with his coffee half a bottle of eau-de-vie into the bargain. Thus satisfied, he has walked all the way to the Avenue de l'Opéra smoking a blond cigar. There, light having suddenly dawned in his brain, he does not take long to recall that having traversed the submarine tunnel at the head of devoted friends, he has conquered England, and is now going to marry the daughter of a Saxon king, who is flying with her swan's wings, and that the wedding celebrations will last for sixty days, during which roast venison will be eaten, and entire oxen served on golden plates.

Raising his eyes, Robert Vic cannot doubt that he will be king, for the heavens are already extending saffron, scarlet and crimson carpets joyfully for him; cloudy actors are performing Shakespeare's tragedies there, and, mounted on their hippogriffs, warriors in bronze armor are breaking lances in his honor. Thinking about future battles and great feasts, Robert experiences a need to lean on a shoulder, to recount his joy to someone and to oppress a resigned confidant. To talk to the houses seems to him to be rather grandiose, and he thinks about it at first, but the houses, prey to a furious dementia, flee frantically, and, like the gas-lamps, the trams, the omnibuses and even the fiacres, are carried away with a diabolical rapidity.

The student tries in vain to arrest them and take them to the police station; they do not stop, and vanish into the vague horizon. The chimneys, the roofs, the sky and the clouds, driven by a stinging whip, also fly away, and the passers-by, projected into the distance, fly away like arrows launched by a solid bow.

However, Robert ends up catching up with one of them. Without being astonished by his uniform and the bayonet hanging from his belt, he seizes him, lifts him up like a child in his Herculean arms and clutches him preciously to his bosom, like a Nymph with her basket of flowers, He runs too, like the gas-lamps and the houses, and carries the *sergent de ville* to the nearest police station.

LXXXII
INTERIOR

The poet Henri Zandre had gone to spend a few days in the country and said that he would not return home before the first of August. But in the morning of the twenty-eighth of July he felt such a need to see his house, his books and the poems he had commenced again that he quit Barbizon and the forest abruptly. He has just come back and is getting ready to open the windows, like Hernani in the fifth act, when he hears the tumult and noise of a strange hubbub.

In fact, counting on his absence, the inhabitants of the house are having a good time, without any concern for his decency, entirely at their ease. A Chinese poet painted on the enamel lamp, clad in crepe robes with an excess of pale lilac silk, with a ruby button on his skull-cap, has descended, and is sitting on a cushion writing verses with his brush. Japanese ladies in numerous robes and tortoiseshell pins have quit the crepes and are chatting under the curtains lifted up by golden cords. The flowers of the nacarat Utrecht velvet garnishing the furniture have slid out of the fabric and have started blooming in the carpet. From a silk painting a river has launched forth, the waves of which, traced in dry golden lines, are inhabited by green fish, and that river is flowing past a red tortoiseshell bookcase. Emerging from an engraving taken from Watteau, the Amintes, Églés and Silvandres of the Enchanted Isle are chatting beside the lake and the tranquil mountains, which have also become real, and looking anxiously at fairground idlers; and women in brightly colored dresses by Robida, who have escaped from the paper on which they were illustrated, leading the lives of Polichinelles and carriage-shafts.

A great cutlass, quitting its scabbard, is planted in the parquet, and a bandit's head sculpted in the cedar-wood that forms its hilt is opening its mouth and respiring avidly. The brass lion that marches over rocks dragging a golden ball under its foot and bearing a tambour on its back that contains a clock, on which a bird is perched, lying in ambush behind a garland of flowers, is strolling around the room with all is baggage, and the lion is roaring and the bird is singing, with long chimes. And the bronze satyresses bearing the contorted branches of chandeliers are dancing, agitating their caprine legs lasciviously.

When Zandre opens his window, all those persons hasten to resume their places, meekly returning to the ideal life. Only his brother, the Chinese poet, has to be begged. He climbs on to the mantelpiece, cursing, but before flattening himself in the milky background of the lamp, amid the aquamarine foliage, he says to Henri Zandre in a reproachful tone:

"You said that you wouldn't be back so soon. I haven't finished the poem destined for my beloved, but you're going to celebrate Mademoiselle Juliette in yours, whom you won't even be able to compare to starry white jasmine flowers!"

LXXXIII
IN THE WOOD

Queen Titania is lying on a bed of moss in the depths. of the wood, and asleep at her feet is the beautiful Indian child that she has not wanted to give to Oberon in order that he might make him his page. Over the head of the great Fay, branches charged with flowers bend down, which, when she pushes them away, fill the air with their divine aromas. But suddenly, in those very flowers, in the red and pink calices and the twigs that support them, she hears the faint rolling of thousands and thousands of little drums. It is all the little Sylphs, who are advancing over the branches in battle order, with little regimental drums on their midriffs, clad in beautiful yellow copper, hanging from their necks on ratskin bandoliers, and they are beating marches with a savage enthusiasm.

"What is it?" says Titania. "Can't you let me sleep?"

"Deferentially, great Queen," says the little spirit Dewdrop, doing her best to imitate the bold tone of the one known as Pitou, "I beg Your Majesty's pardon, but there's no means of sleeping. And this morning it's necessary that we make a noise, and all the thunder of an earthquake, because General Farre[1] is being buried, and the drums have been repaired."

---

1 Jean-Joseph Farre (1816-1887) was a general during the Franco-Prussian War and later served as Minister of War during the Third Republic; he was still alive when this vignette was published and very active in the Senate, where he routinely voted with the left and generated protest when he successfully proposed the suppression of drums in the Army.

LXXXIV
LEAD SOLDIERS

Blowing into her black clarion, the sinister goddess War, armored in scales, has soared in the somber sky. Shells have eviscerated the houses and smashed the villages. The inhabitants have been killed, their daughters raped and murdered. The burned ruins are smoking toward the clouds, the roads are full of dead soldiers with hollow eyes and crushed noses. Brilliant with gold and plumes in the wind, the victors are galloping on their rapid horses, the cannons are rolling on their gun-carriages; trucks filled with booty are following the triumphant army, and meanwhile, mad bulls are running through the fields, and flocks of crows can be seen circling, attracted by the odor of blood.

But that beautiful comedy of battle having finished, the toymaker replaces the dead or grievously wounded soldiers in the crucible, and arranges those that are healthy in their box of thin white fir-wood. When he picks up the proud chief, however—the terrible cuirassier with the bald head, whose wrath makes the world shake and who leads everything with a frown of his eyebrows, the man who makes armies march apace and emperors and kings tremble merely at the sound of his spurs—that wily captain jibs and gives signs of wanting to organize a rebellion.

"What!" he says, striking his Jovian pose, "You're putting me into the box too!"

"Yes," says the toymaker, taking hold of him unceremoniously, "I'm putting you into the box too. For if people listened to you, it would never be finished, the shop would never be in order. And don't I have to occupy myself with varnishing my trees, my sheepfolds and my stars?"

EIGHTH DOZEN

LXXXV
REMEMBRANCE

She and He, two Souls, two Clarities, two blessed Spirits, Théro and Celmis, clad in their giant grace, united and supporting one another, narrowly entwined, are advancing at a rhythmic pace, floating through the bright paradise. They have traversed the diamond city whose tangled spires and high forests of violets, and the mild river as wide as twenty oceans, along the shore that is planted with a single rose-bush, whose branches charged with flowers shelter the vast waves in their shade. Gently stimulated by the resonance of subtle perfumes and silent music, they are now in a large clearing, from which they can perceive in the infinite ether all the flocks of constellations of stars.

"Wait!" says Celmis. "Look at that very tiny and fugitive spark in the distance. That's the Earth. Do you remember that we once lived there? Yes, many thousands and thousands of centuries before the sacred and triumphal hour, overflowing with joy, when we finally saw, burning with delight in the ecstasy of light, THAT which cannot be expressed even by celestial words; before we had inhabited, incessantly renewed, rejuvenated and magnified, so many planets and stars; before the long persistence of a mutual amour had rendered us exactly similar to one another, so that my face reflects yours like a mirror, and the eyes of the Angels cannot tell our thoughts and the flames of our hair apart; yes, well before that, we lived on that tiny distant and vague dot; and we even experienced, I still remember, something named Suffering—but I can no longer remember what it was."

LXXXVI
THE TREE

The tree is condemned, because it has grown much too close to the house, in which it causes damp. It is an enormous pine, straight and magnificent, with yellowing bark, whose branches are as horizontal as those of a cedar, and whose somber verdure is mingled with its cones, also green. But it is too close to the house, it must die, and here comes the executioner. It is Père Pédroleau, a very old woodcutter, who does not sleep in his bedroom twice a year, who always stays in the forest, and who resembles an old tree himself. For fifty years he has not done anything else but fell trees; his pallor is green-tinted; his beard, trimmed like that of a Greek chieftain before Ilios, has taken on the appearance of foliage and moss, and his resolute, terribly clear eyes are like escapees from heaven into the forest.

After having marked by eye from the nearby meadow the place where the pine is going to fall, Pédroleau attacks it with great blows of the ax. Opening sure cuts, lifting away morsels of flesh with an absolute precision; the soul of the pine moans, cries and laments horribly, but the pitiless old man keeps on striking. Soon, the maddened tree raises its arms desperately one last time and, launched into the air, comes to fall exactly in the place Pédroleau has chosen. And the old man, bitten and slapped so many times by the storms, by the wind and by the frost, is as straight as the old tree with the somber foliage had been just now, and like the tree, he is waiting, his feet pinned to the ground, for the fatal moment, for the other woodcutter and the inevitable ax.

LXXXVII
IDYLL

The geese are walking in a flock, irregularly, raising their orange beaks, sketching movements the reason for which they have immediately forgotten, and making chimerical plans to pass through the well-blocked hedges. Behind them, in the full glare of the sun, tanned, tawny and superbly illuminated, comes the little goose-girl, clad in worn rags, as blue and straight as an I, without any of what makes the visible glory of a woman, and yet noble and hieratic by virtue of the very simplicity of her construction.

She is so thin and so straight that she could serve as a theme for an I in one of those newspapers of images that commence all their articles with ornamental letters. Her bare feet are shining in the sand of the road, as yellow as topazes; her colorless lips are smiling vaguely, and her supernaturally bright eyes, as clear and profound as a pale sky, are fixed on her animals. She is pushing the white-plumaged geese, as primal and majestic as a goose herself, and before her, as if to celebrate her infantile beauty, above a heap of stones erected by the administration of bridges and highways, a lark flies up and rises into the charmed air, hectically modulating its pretty triumphant song.

LXXXVIII
ANOTHER DON JUAN

He has stolen his agile grace from a cat, and his fine black hair and moustache from a pug. From a king he has taken a piece of his crimson robe, from a Jew a piece of his yellow robe, and from spring a piece of her green robe, and with the fragments he has made the coat of an ape, which clings to his gracious stolen body. He has put in his red leather belt a club covered in fine white skin, and before striking, tickling and caressing, his red shoes, in which there must be quicksilver, relentlessly trace the image of a frantic song, and an undulating and various hat, which changes shape incessantly, is carved from a cloud.

That is why, served like a king and as clever as a Jew, always as young as immortal April in flower, he flees through cities and through verdure, amorously followed by Colombes and white Columbines, who, seeing that he has the wherewithal to stun them, dazzle them and beat them, adore that horrible and charming monster. He, meanwhile, fluttering like a hideous butterfly with beautiful wings, embraces them with his flexible arm; he amuses them, courts them, caresses them and beats them, and draws them into his vertiginous dance amid enchanted and conquered nature; he makes them kiss his muzzle of a black dog—and he is Arlequin!

LXXXIX
THE FLOCK

Lined up, conducted by nuns as yellow as ivory, the orphan girls clad in their violet-striped robes pass by, coiffed in linen bonnets and wearing medals on broad blue ribbons around their necks. Long, masculine, as straight as sticks, tanned and kissed by the shadow, the wind and the sun, they resemble boys, because they have not been educated in charm and because they are too poor and disinherited to have learned grace. Only one among them, by virtue of some absurd and crazy jest of destiny, is as beautiful as a young queen, curvaceous and with imperious and divine features, like a wild lily that has grown in a field of rye.

XC
SCIENTIA

Already weary of the struggle, emaciated, pale and jaundiced, the artist Paul Héras is lying in a large tapestry armchair. He senses that malady has touched him with its cruel finger, and yet he would like to live, for his dear faithful wife and for his children, who still need to eat. Opposite him astride a chair, chattering and admiring himself, is his physician Guy de Macroton, young, flighty, world-weary, well-dressed and charming. His coiffure, in which, like Caussidière,[1] he has made order with disorder, is a masterpiece; his light beard flutters around his pink face; his suit, made of soft cloth, through which run pale blue stripes and imperceptible rose-red stripes, makes him resemble a damsel-fly. Guy is smoking an improbably enormous greenish yellow cigar that similarly seems fatigued by vigils, and he is gazing at his patient with an indifference that, by dint of its intensity, becomes touching.

"Well, dear friend, what can you do for me?" said Paul Héras, sadly.

"Pooh!" says the young practitioner disdainfully. "Between us, my dear, hygiene, cares and distraction, that's the foun-

---

1 The oft-imprisoned political agitator Marc Caussidière (1808-1861) played a prominent part in the 1848 Revolution and was appointed prefect of police under the subsequent provisional government; he attempted to carry out a sweeping reorganization of police forces in Paris but was soon dismissed, and was then forced to flee to the USA, but he returned to France in 1859, taking advantage of an amnesty offered to exiles and refugees by Napoléon III.

dation of the matter. However, if you have a taste for some medication, don't be embarrassed. Bromide and salicylate are very fashionable, and I know honest people who are mad for injections of morphine. Or have you a desire to go to some thermal waters? Oh, my God, it doesn't matter which; I'm not here to contradict you. But before going, you must come to my house-warming, the inauguration of my little town house. Oh dear, what amour! Not a stick of furniture, nothing but paintings, tapestries, screens and incense-burners. And I receive my patients, not in a study cluttered with books, but in an apple-green boudoir where there's an aquarium with pink glass, with Chinese fish, and that's modern enough. Yes, you must come, unless in the meantime... but, in fact, why the devil shouldn't you be cured? Maladies aren't always as nasty as they're made out to be, and there's no reason why they can't be cured... if they're let alone!"

XCI
THE LITTLE FRIEND

As the poet Raoul Tavan still had three sous he bought a small loaf of overcooked bread, quite burned, and from the pork-butcher's copper box, as brilliant as the shield of Telamonian Ajax, he chose a hot sausage; then he savored that satisfying meal in the street while walking. Now, in order to have the pleasure of drink, he has installed himself in front of a Wallace fountain[1] and he holds out the metal cup under the bright thread of running water. But in that trickle of water, iridescent in the sunlight, a little Naiad has suddenly appeared, pale, thin, anemic and very Parisienne, with bleary eyes, slightly ashamed of her lead shoes, who murmurs and whispers beautifully scanned rhymes to the poet. Raoul Tavan drinks the cup of water and goes away, sated, and happy, master of the world—for he has the wherewithal in his pocket to make a very small cigarette—while through the holes in his shoes, torn and gaping, an errant breeze is caressing his light feet and refreshing them delectably.

---

1 The English philanthropist Sir Richard Wallace decided, while Paris was being rebuilt after the damage inflicted on it by the Prussian artillery during the siege of 1870, to finance the construction of a number of elaborate public drinking fountains. In one of the models the water emerged from the mouth of a sculpted naiad.

XCII
SOUTHERNERS

Buried in the silky waves of his beard and black hair, the very small Marius Cabardos is sitting at a table where he has just devoured an entire cassoulet, a pot of goose confit and a bowl of fruits and berberis jam, all washed down with generous wines and golden muscats. He has eaten alone, served by three magnificent giantesses, who resemble city statues, Aminte and Laure with black hair, and Hersilie, as red as a sunset. Hersilie pours eau-de-vie slowly into his coffee, while Aminte presses a long Turkish pipe to her lips, on which Laure places and ember, and as soon as it is well alight, they hold it out to the young sultan.

Between Cabardos père, merchant of oils in Cintegabelle, and Joséphin Gabarou, draper, it has been agreed that Marius Cabardos will marry one of the demoiselles Gabarou, and Marius has been sent to Toulouse to the home of old Joséphin to make his choice. By a bizarre caprice of amour, the three giantesses have immediately fallen madly in love with the somber dwarf, and that is why they are serving him like faithful slaves.

But Joséphin Gabarou has come in. With a gesture, he sends away those superb lovers and remains alone with Marius.

"Well, dear boy," he says to him. "I think that you've studied my daughters enough now. So, which do you prefer? I'll give her to you."

"Hmm!" grunts Marius, making a ferocious moue and spitting out a flood of smoke, which enters his beard and exits again in thin blue threads. "Your daughters? Oh well! I'll tell you: I couldn't give a damn about one of them as easily as another."

XCIII
FALSE EXIT

In the depths of the Thébaide, on a mountain, in his hut of mud and reeds, Saint Antoine is asleep momentarily, and so is the pig. When they both wake up, the cabin has been replaced by a vast mixture of gardens and buildings, in which gold, marble and porphyry, white nudities and triumphant flowers shine. Perforated facades, pilasters and audacious stairways launch forth in the open air, and lilacs, giant rose-bushes and immense lilies are flourishing, at the same time as the fruit-trees and the vines are succumbing under the weight of ripe fruits. And all that is full of naked women with voluptuous rednesses, who are showing off their immodest bodies in a thousand lascivious poses. Some, hanging on to marble balconies, terminate in arabesques of living flowers; others, in the water, germinate in piscine tails, and all of them are singing and smiling, disheveled, and illuminating the air with their fiery eyes. Clad only in hunting-waistcoats, naked huntresses are piercing prey with their arrows; others are angling for monstrous fish in lakes, and female cooks, with no other garment than a waistcoat as white as snow, are preparing victuals.

The tables of the feast extend as far as the eye can see, surrounded by furious dances, and, knowing that ugliness is immoral, other demons are displaying pointed and horned heads, absurdly long noses and the abdomens of crabs, while a thousand impure animals are swarming in mud, and thousands of vermilion and rose-colored birds are soaring in the air.

A beautiful queen, whose open chemise allows her pointed breasts to be seen and whose robe of tinsel and gems is being carried by a page, approaches the saint and offers him a foaming cup. But without allowing himself to be astonished, he says a prayer in a loud voice. Immediately, like a heap of dry leaves swept away by a hurricane, the trees, the perforated palaces and the mad women are carried away by the reckless wind, and the cleansed cabin recovers its ordinary aspect.

But a poor little green devil, still young and innocent, has not been quick enough. He is caught by the door, which has slammed violently, and already, Saint Antoine's companion is nibbling his calves with an evident satisfaction. The saint makes every effort, and with his vigorous arm he frees the young devil, who flees, uttering a frightful howl, because, in the meantime, the worthy pig has eaten his tail.

XCIV
ZIMRI

Angèle Riffi has invited her best friends to come and wish her a happy birthday. They are all there, the pick of the crop, Arlès, Madriat, Louis de Triger, Comte Dindo and the rest. But she has given them such a good dinner, with real *coulis*, and the boudoir is so warm, so well illuminated and so comfortable, and everyone is so relaxed there in Japanese satin armchairs, cushions with golden flowers and Persian rugs, that those messieurs, too contented, not even thinking yet about taking from their pockets the jewel-cases they have brought, are selfishly smoking the golden cigars offered by the mistress of the house, and stupidly talking Arabian politics and Egyptian affairs like doorkeepers. Meanwhile, the little dog Zimri, whose master, the painter Joseph Croix has been given permission to bring him, and who has also dined like a diplomat; the strange little Zimri with the head of a Chimera, whose diffuse gaze searches infinity and whose wispy moustache, which he bears between his two eyes, seems to have been made with a beard of feathers grilled in an oven; the eccentric Zimri, deaf in one ear, shows himself go be profoundly irritated by such bourgeois conversations. After having barked furiously, he leaps on to Angèle's knees, then climbs further, and resolutely sets about caressing, kissing and licking the charmer's naked breasts with his long pink tongue.

"Damn it, Zimri!" cries Joseph Croix, in an angry voice, in order to bring the audacious animal back to a stricter observation of decency.

"No, let him," says the beautiful Angèle. And she adds mildly, indicating the little dog: "Monsieur seems to me to be the only one who, for the moment, gets the point."

XCV
THE PAUPERESS

The beautiful Comtesse Josèphe de Lammers is walking beside her lover, Raoul de Sima, in a somber pathway in the Bois, where, through the black foliage, the sun can be seen fleeing behind coppery and violet bands in the red and pink sky. Their footfalls are making the dry leaves squeak; the young man speaks at rare intervals in an emotional and virile voice, but his mistress is chiding him and quarreling with him in haughty, urgent and rapid speech. Madame de Lammers has accorded Raoul one of those rare rendezvous for which he is so avid, but that is not to hear him talk about amour; it is to harass him under the most frivolous pretexts, and to stick a thousand needles of cruel irony into his heart. It is sufficient to look at the two of them to see that the young man is perfectly innocent and that the lady is taking pleasure in torturing him, but the more he protests his honest fidelity, the more she heaps him with random inventions, blinding him with her golden eyes and the pink pallor of her malicious smile.

At that moment, a woman clad almost in rags and coiffed with a kerchief appears on the path, who has evidently been beautiful once, fêted and adored, but has fallen violently into the Hell of poverty. She sees the scene and marches straight up to Madame de Lammers.

"Ah," she says to her, with the frightful serenity of those who know everything, "don't torment a man who loves you like that! Life is so short, and one imagines that it will never end. I too have had men kneeling before me, and amour; I imagined that the amour wouldn't be used up, and would always be there. I didn't care about it, I disdained it, I pursed my lips, but now—I'd take it from a head afflicted with ringworm!"

XCVI
THE FEAST

On an immense table, the ends of which cannot be seen, the feast is served on a snow-white tablecloth where crystal and silverware are shining, with gold decorations representing hunts, dancing fêtes and the wars of the gods of Olympus. Sitting between women with bare breasts, the guests are eating and devouring. In front of them pyramids of flowers and fruits rise up, and to satisfy their hunger, venison and pork on golden platters, roasted peacocks, monstrous fish, green and pink sauces, and pâtés like citadels, with towers, cannons and drawbridges. Joints of meat are fuming on trays, and yet the cries, horns and halloos of hunters can be heard outside, who are killing yet more game to put in place of those.

Beautiful naked girls, around whom a light drapery of scarlet silk is floating, are holding torches; master-chefs are cutting up meat on golden tables; a thousand valets are hastening back and forth, and the service is provided by long-haired pages. Music, songs and dances glimpsed in the distance enliven the repast, and sometimes a poet gets to his feet, picks up his lute, and recites some glorious poem, to which the guests listen with transports of joy. Sometimes, too, on a tray studded with diamonds and sapphires, a naked woman is served on a bed of flowers, and immediately carried away as soon as eyes have been sated by her irreproachable beauty. And still the feast continues and the thin iridescent glasses are emptied and filled.

From time to time, a pale woman crowned with blue-tinted verdure appears at one of the doors. Silently, she makes a sign, and several guests, usually old men with white hair, but also women and men of the most various ages, get up and follow her. They never come back, and are never seen again; but in their places children with avid gazes come to sit down, with hair over their eyes, who plunge their hands in the dishes, bite their neighbors' breasts and smear themselves with cream.

NINTH DOZEN

XCVII
FANFRELUCHE

The thinnest, the most delicate, the sleekest and the most impalpable of Parisiennes, after and perhaps before—the one that everyone admires, the divine Luce Dam—is strolling, surrounded by her court in the pathways of the Jardin d'Acclimation. She is as white as a sheet of nacre, as pink as a rose of Bengal, crowned with hair quivering like molten gold that has been thrown into cold water. And magnificently dressed! For, knowing that over her body, as smooth and uniform as an ivory wand, no indiscreet inequality will hinder the flight of their fancy, the fabrics, the satins, the plushes, the ecstatic and rich damasks yield to their joy, quivering and inflating in the wind, fall back in cascades, rise up in bold stairways, or fly away, as in those seventeenth-century portraits in which seigneurs and financiers are sumptuously displayed even in the accessories lavished around their images.

Luce is carrying on her fist the little white dog Fanfreluche, as big as a mouse. That futile animal is adorned with a silver plate collar bordered with yellow diamonds, on which a patient engraver has represented Nymphs in the woods of Taygête, the tower of the lake in the Bois de de Boulogne, the triumph of Bakkhos on his return from India, and the clowns of the Folies-Bergère.

From time to time Luce utters a little pearly laugh, or throws out some meaningless phrase, or a simple interjection, and the seigneurs and seigneuresses who are following her swoon as if they had just heard a new song by Mozart. Finally, they arrive at the amusing animals; the slender sovereign declares that she wants to mount the elephant, and to ride it on her own. She is, in fact, hoisted up into the palanquin, like a light feather to the top of a citadel, and the contrast is so raw and violent that the bourgeois strollers are stupefied by it.

But then comes another, which no one is expecting. As ironic as an aged Parisian, the wily elephant makes a semblance of panting, buckling and succumbing under the frivolous burden. He mimes his scene as the great Deburau[1] might have done, simulating struggles, contortions and desperate efforts, finally falling to his knees, as if he can go no further, and then getting up and setting off at a gallop, in order to show that all that was nothing but a game and a joke.

"My dear," says Maride to his friend Bergeron, "that is an animal who makes quips like you and me. In order to make a good and beautiful epigram, it's sufficient to know, like a Boileau,[2] how to ornament it with two rhymes.

"And it isn't even necessary to link them," said Bergeron, "for the elephant, so kind to little children, can do anything it wants in performance, and it possesses thoroughly the instinct of order and symmetry that is the essential characteristic of a poet."

1 The celebrated mime Jean-Gaspard Deburau (1796-1846), the star of the Théâtre des Fuambules for the last thirty years of his life, who appeared under the name Baptiste, usually costumed as Pierrot, in which guise he became an archetype beloved by the member of the Romantic Movement, whose significance was inherited by the Panassians and the Symbolists, and who is featured more than once in the present collage.
2 The poet and purist critic Nicolas Boileau-Despréaux (1636-1711), who published a controversial but influential analysis of *L'Art poétique* (1674).

XCVIII
CHILDISHNESS

Two invalids, Sergeant Picquenard and his comrade Gachet, are walking outside their lodgings under a torrid July sunlight, which would be sufficient to roast lizards and cook them thoroughly, but which warms the blood of the worthy old men agreeably. Picquenard was sixteen years old in 1798, when he first took up arms in the capture of Fribourg under Maréchal Brune. Today he is a centenarian; his toothless and hairless head has become as black as that of a mulatto; his eyebrows are as long and thick as brushwood, and his real leg has become so similar to his wooden leg that one can no longer tell them apart. Charred in Egypt, adored in Germany, shot in Spain, frozen in Russia, the infantryman with the skin of a crocodile has been tanned and goffered sufficiently to live forever. The profound scar that bisects his face has blanched and faded, and memories, legends and dreams are mixed up confusedly in his old noggin. Gachet, an alert one-armed man who is a child by comparison with him—for he is no more than seventy years old—is listening to his superior with all military respect, and also with the naïve ingenuousness of a Jocrisse.

"Yes, my lad," Picquenard continues, "as I told you, I was in bed with my shoes and everything, on a white satin couch, and the Princess of Cyprus was pouring me wine from a golden jug. Then she put her arms around my neck and she said: 'Don't go, or I'll do something desperate; I'll open the window and throw myself into the sea.'"

"And you, sergeant," says the eager Gachet, "what did you say to that?"

"Me," says Picquenrd, smacking his black lips, "I said to her: 'Little mother, amour and all that is very nice, but I have to go and conquer cities, and if I amuse myself with trivia like an idler, instead of entering into capitals, who would thumb their nose? It would be the Emperor.'"

XCIX
IMITATION OF AESOP

The indefatigable musician, the octogenarian swan Tizoles, is surrounded by women, nymphs and girls in his pretty town house in the Rue Saint-Georges, the drawing rooms of which, the gold and the hangings, have grown old with him, and like him they defend themselves, a heap of faded things but young and charming. The master is young too, or, at least would be if he did not cut his side-whiskers, shaped like those of Monsieur Scribe, and the petty people who surround him laugh, babble and swarm, a winged flock of Song and Dance, Alidas, Antys, Michelin Is and Goguelu IIs, throw over his pale face the pink and crimson reflection of a hundred red mouths. Drunk on perfumes, amiable voices and living flesh, Tizoles remembers amours, green by-ways trodden and the intoxication of twenty years of age, the two-sou eclogues and the paths of Meudon. *And when I say Meudon, suppose Tivoli!*

All of that he remembers so clearly that he wants to recount it to little Morize; to bring her half-way into his memories and his causes, he takes her into the little neighboring boudoir hung in pink, the white carpet of which has been brushed, forty years earlier, by the light feet of Fanny Ellsler.[1] But at the redoubtable moment, the fellow senses such an implacable chill running through his veins that he is alarmed and cannot articulate a word. It is in vain that he strives; bitter winter is

---

1 Fanny Elssler (1810-1884) was an Austrian ballerina much admired by Théophile Gautier when she performed at the Paris Opéra.

trembling and moaning within him, and in his despair, Tizoles does what Aesop's woodcutter does and summons Death to his aid.

She comes, but smiling, dolled-up and softened. She is a comic opera Death, with a pretty wig on her cranium, rouge on her skeletal cheeks and a pale flower in her corsage. She is enveloped by a light veil, ornamented with jewelry and carefully made-up, for she does not want to frighten an Epicurean whom everyone loves so dearly, and who loves himself just as much.

"Here I am," she says. "What do you want with me?"

"Me?" replies Tizoles, violently surprised and showing her little Morize, with embarrassment. "I want you to help me to…"

"Oh, I beg your pardon," murmurs the visitor, who is already fleeing. "I don't get mixed up with that: quite the contrary!"

C
DISHONEST PROPOSITION

With his indefatigable guide with the light curly beard and the brown face, who is leading him over the chamois paths, the poet Josz has arrived, exhausted and bloodied but drunk on space and pure air, at the summit of the high mountain. The two travelers have the pride of victory in their faces; eagles are flying above their heads and clouds are accumulated beneath their feet, already full of the frightful breath of the tempest. At that moment Josz sees that, from the brown that he was, his guide has become quite black, with eyes as red as embers and phosphorescent gleams in his hair. That bizarre companion is smiling in the most engaging fashion, but showing little teeth as delectably green as the first tender leaves of spring.

"Yes," he says, "don't be astonished; I am, in fact, the Devil. Look down below in the vague distance, at the fields, the cities, and the towns: at the absurd human forest. Would you like all there is within it: gold, palaces, repose, luxury, parks full of shade and fresh waters, marvelously beautiful women, dressed and ornamented as you wish, as complicated as Chinese puzzles, and glory, and laurels, the Académie, the editors of the *Journal des Débats* and the *Revue des Deux Mondes* kissing your knees, the Comédie-Française belonging to you, like the house of Orgon to Tartuffe? It's very easy!"

"But then," says Josz, "what would it cost me?"

"Oh, almost nothing," replies the Devil. "It's only a matter of writing verses like…"

"Like who?" asks Josz, in a firm voice, looking the Devil straight in the eyes.

The tempter is visibly embarrassed; he dare not pronounce the indecent word. However, he does what devotees do who profit from the moment when Monsieur le Curé blows his nose; he seizes a moment when the storm-wind is blowing with all its force, lightning is furrowing the sky and thunder is bursting forth loudly, and in the midst of the tumult of the unleashed elements, he timidly pronounces the abominable name.

"Well, no," says the poet, "that's too dear; I prefer the periodicals that don't pay, bedrooms in which it rains, initial women and wooden steaks."

CI
THE ACTOR

The room is both a study and a dressing-room. On the wall, panoplies are hung over the severe wallpaper, colossal swords from all ages, and numerous portraits representing the same figure in various costumes, their sumptuous frames crowned with silver and gold, with long ribbons, souvenirs of triumphs obtained in Liège, in Castelnaudary, in Nice and other cities.

Negligently thrown on a tapestry armchair are a black velvet costume and a plumed hat, and pell-mell, on a Renaissance table, a volume of Molière, a bound copy of *La Tour de Nesle*, and various manuscript roles, all belonging to plays by William Busnach.[1] On a set of shelves, at least forty pairs of boots of different sizes are aligned, which seem nevertheless to belong to the same man, as if he sometimes had big feet and sometimes small ones, at the whim of certain particular conveniences.

Sitting quite alone, Montferrat, the greatest of leading actors, is prey to a terrible dolor. His features are convulsed, moans and sobs are elevating his bosom, and large ears are falling from his bloodshot eyes and running into his black moustache. The actor is sitting before a dressing-table covered in bottles, paints, brushes, cosmetics, stumps, pastel pencils, entirely shaken and harassed by the most genuine despair there ever was, but occupied nevertheless in painting his face. He is

---

1 The dramatist William Busnach (1832-1907), director of the Théâtre de l'Athénée after 1867, whose greatest successes were adaptations of novels by Émile Zola.

putting burnt umber on his eyelids, extinguishing with white greasepaint the redness of his mouth; he is designing with a bold stroke a wrinkle that will cause his lips to fall, and at intervals he gives a desolate and stiff movement to his long hair. At the same time, he does not cease groaning, bowled over by an emotion that subdues and crushes him like a tree felled by a storm wind.

The comic Blime has entered in tiptoe. Bald, clean-shaven and resigned, his soft gaze and pale lips express the generous affection of an honest man.

"What are you doing?" he asks the great leading man.

"You can see, old man," says Montferrat, sobbing more forcefully, simultaneously throwing a decisive feature on his cheeks with a stump. "I'm 'making my head'—to go to my brother's funeral."

CII
THE LUXEMBOURG

To the wood I shall go alone; Amour will count me there. Crazy, disheveled, ingenuous roses, little girls are dancing rounds and singing *Giroflé, girofla!*—and it is a joy to see them, fresher than the other flowers that ornament the Luxembourg gardens, where the air is full of perfumes. From far away the chords arrive of the military band, which is playing a triumphal march, and the two musics do not embarrass one another—on the contrary. There is a little girl who is leading the dance, whose profound eyes resemble violets. The grenadiers, whose drums, hidden by the terrace, cannot be seen, make their crimson flowers burst forth; nearby, the oleanders flourish in clumps as on the bank of a celestial stream, and the plumage of swans is resplendent in the sunlight.

Amour will count me there. It does indeed count there. A young newly-married couple, equally infatuated and beautiful, stop to watch the dance, and already, with the instinct of maternity in her heart, the adored young woman is admiring and counting the girls red with pleasure and coiffed with blonde fleeces, who will later go, one by one, to the wood where the stream murmurs and the turtle-doves moan.

Ceyras, the illustrious old mathematician, who has lifted all veils but who, devoted to bitter and divine Science, has never been a father, has also stopped to listen to the song: *If you encounter Amour there, Giroflé, Girofla…!* He listens to the

pink girls, then sighs and draws away, and, his eyes fixed on
the setting sun in the great bloodied sky, before walls of copper and citadels of bronze, he gazes, with eyes that pierce the
clouds, at disheveled horses, the clash of arms and the horrible
battles of the gods.

CIII
THE DEVIL'S WIFE

Ordinarily, as everyone knows, the Devil is scarlet from head to toe, like a cardinal in a clinging robe, whose face might have been tailored in the same cloth from which his garments had been taken. But at the present moment he is as red as the embers in the hearth, an intense, plushy, pink and whitening red, and his lip is fuming like a hot-plate, because his wife is pulling him vertiginously with an incredible expenditure of force, by his long forked tail, which passes over his correct waistcoat— the only one of our garments that the Devil, refractory to other items of our costume, consents to adopt. He, the scarlet Devil, and she, his wife—clad in the latest Parisienne fashion, it is true, in a dress whose fabric is blazing fire—are both bent double, he forwards, trying to escape, she backwards and still tugging, offering the spectacle of a terribly united household.

"It's too much, it's too much!" says the poor flamboyant fellow, finally, crimson and charred, sweating effortfully. "Let me breathe, for mercy's sake!"

"Ah! says the lady, pulling harder than ever, "Be just, my friend! We can't live on the flame of time; my household doesn't run on nothing, and the domestics have become impossible, as you know. To maintain your useful relations with the other Hells and to satisfy the ministers that represent them, as well as the diplomatic corps, it's necessary that I give a few dinners from time to time. Now, I can offer those people fillets mummified by the Swiss method, fake *foie gras* fabricated in prisons, and wines whose bouquet and aroma are imitated in accordance with the method taught at the Institute of Klusternenberg[1] in Austria in vain; I still can't make ends meet. Not to mention my Saturday receptions and my five o'clock teas, where Mesdames the Demonesses consume less tea than picrate.

"In sum, my friend, you're the Devil, and given the cost of wages, chambermaids, lovers, vegetables and black dresses from our couturier Nessus, and butter—even margarine—what can I do in order not to pull the Devil by the tail?"

---

1 I have rendered this name as it is given in the original, but it might be misprinted there; the intended reference is surely to Klosterneuberg, the location of a famous monastery.

CIV
THE GOOD HUNTER

In the pretty dining-room of his property of Les Clochettes, sitting at a table sculpted in the time of François I, around which a garland of vines runs and intertwines, old Père Loze, while awaiting the real repast, is having a little snack. Under his knife a disemboweled fortress made of creamed pears is collapsing and gradually diminishing, and, lifting his broad-bellied demijohn, which holds five or six liters, he is frequently filling his enormous glass of engraved crystal, worthy of being compared with Bassompierre's boot.[1]

"Well, my dear neighbor," his young friend Jean Saphore says to the old man as he comes in, "how are you this morning?"

"As you can see," says Père Loze, thin and tanned like Cordovan leather, superb in his hunting costume, "I'm still fresh and I carry my eighty-three years well. Although I've lost three fingers in battle, I'm sure enough of my rifle-shot, and yesterday, with my worthy dog Darius, I killed six partridges and two hares in the thicket of Chantelaube. I have good feet, good eyes and the appetite persists; there's only one thing that is no longer going very well, and that's women. I don't know why."

---

1 There is a famous engraving dating from 1852 of a cartoon depicting Maréchal François de Bassimpière (1579-1646) drinking from his "cauldron boot."

CV
CONFESSION

About two o'clock in the morning, at Hill's, Séraphine Disse is sitting at a table all alone, expressly alone. She is eating Indian pickles with mustard, like red octopodes, and from time to time an entire crayfish with the carapace, which she crunches with her little canine teeth, all mingled with a few cigarettes. And she is drinking a terrible beverage like the black water of the Cocytus, mixed according to her instructions, which burns the glass.

"I've finally found you!" says young Émile Pommera, who has come in, pale as linen and has sat down next to the young woman. "Oh, Séraphine, love me, and love me faithfully, for if I don't possess you, for myself alone, I shall die of despair, having all the infernos in my breast!"

Séraphine is blonde and pretty, fleshy, with a hint of Hollandaise, impudently pink; her gray and green eyes are a cerulean color, and her musical voice resonates with an abominable accuracy.

"Well," she says, "you interest me, in sum. I'll show you my heart, such as it is—if it is a heart! I love evil, without passion, for I don't experience any passion, but with an obstinate apathy. I'm treacherous for the sake of treachery; I don't say or want to say a word that isn't a lie; two brothers, who were my lovers, have killed one another for love of me, and that doesn't even upset me. I wake up asking myself what I can do that's cruel and absurd, and I do it, joylessly, with a glacial cold, uniquely by virtue of depravity. And that, my dear friend, is the pretty little woman you desire."

"Oh, no," murmurs Émile in a stifled and tremulous voice. "Tell me that you wanted to frighten me, and that all that is a dream, a lie, a frightful comedy!"

"Well," says Séraphine Disse, making her decision, with the exasperated fatigue of an actress putting in her rouge for the hundred thousandth time, "you're right, Émile. All that is only a game, and I'm joking." And she adds, with a wicked smile: "The truth is that I love you—and I'll be completely faithful to you."

CVI
JUST REWARD

Young Roger Pierril has come to see his illustrious master, Castri, of whom it can be said that he is a great poet, even in the century of Victor Hugo. The youth finds that demigod with the black beard of Olympian Zeus alarmed and amazed, for he is listening to a visitor, Madame Henriette Bouderis of Verdun, come from afar to admire him, whose fabulous discourse is astonishing the man who has been astonishing the world for thirty years.

The provincial lady is a colossus of strength and beauty. Her narrow forehead, devoured by black hair, her bulging eyes, her pitilessly straight nose, her Classical lips and chin, and her neck like a brown ivory tower seem to have been stolen from a museum. It is easy to see that she is not wearing any species of corset, and it would not take much for her pure, turbulent, bold breasts, as rebellious as Spartacus, to pierce her dress.

"Yes," she says, staring into the void, "I wanted to know you because it's so flattering to converse with a witty man. We'll sing ballads and you'll make jokes for me. I know a few too. Do you know which saint has no need of garters?"

Before that supernatural harpy the master remains silent. But Pierril, who divines him and has him at his fingertips, hears him mentally say to the Michelangeloesque idol: "Go on, continue, give yourself to pleasure, be as stupid as a flock of geese. But soon, when the little young man has gone, I'll have my turn; I'll take my revenge with my fingernails, and I'll squeeze you in my arms so long and so hard that you'll no longer be able to say anything at all!"

CVII
AMICUS PLATO

Half-lying on white silk cushion with golden flowers dotted with tender green, Célestine Oddo resembles a goddess far more than a woman; for, in spite of her beautiful flesh, her pallor gives her an immaterial air, and rather than having been bought from a couturier, her soft and floating silver lamé robe appear to have been woven diligently in some paradise.

"There you are," she says to Henri Spever, who enters the obscure little drawing-room timidly. "You accept my conditions, then; how touched and truly proud I am! Ah, my dear, what a joy it is, in fact, to love one another in the silent union of souls, to think that, in order to express the ecstasies that envelop us, even music is too coarse a language, and to savor with their infinite delights sensualities exempt from soiling! Yes, we shall have the ineffable pleasure of adoring one another, and knowing that which we do not say…"

"Yes," Henri responds, "We'll love one another in your fashion." And, opening the silken envelope in which he has brought her a superb cardboard cutlet, a theater prop colored in raw red and yellow tones, he adds in an elegiac tone:

"And afterwards, if we're hungry, we can eat this!"

CVIII
EVERYWOMAN

Under an implacable steely sky, in bare sand where not a blade of grass grows, the bleak, despairing and weary Danaïdes are drawing water from the mute river, relentlessly emptying and filling their urns, trying to fill the bottomless barrels from which the water escapes incessantly, swallowed and drunk by the avid sand. And they are desolate, wringing their hands dolorously, moaning while accomplishing their horrible task. But now, cleaving through the air, a golden-haired winged messenger, more beautiful than Hermes, his face displaying a triumphant pride, alights on the ground nearby. It is the irreproachable Asterius. He makes a sign with his golden wand, and immediately the labor of the wretches ceases to be vain, and the water no longer runs away.

"O dear heads," says the young god, "your woes are over. The Titan-Gods are vanquished; the race of Iapetus and Clymene of the beautiful heels has dethroned its rebel sons, and Prometheus, liberated from his chains, has quit the black rock where the vulture was devouring his liver. Your torture is finished, and look, the barrels are full!"

He has spoken, but the Danaïdes, Hippomedusa, Glaucippe, Celeno, Stygne, Anymone and their other sisters, far from letting their joy burst forth, look at one another with confused and disappointed expressions. Finally, Neso breaks the silence first.

"The barrels are full?" she says, caressing her red hair sadly. "Well, what are we going to do now?"

TENTH DOZEN

CIX
THE LABORER

She has dug a large and immense hole in the soft earth, which she is hollowing out briskly with her skeletal fingers, and, inclining her perforated torso and her bare white skull, She heaps up in that abyss, pale and cold, old and young men, women and rigid children, whose eyelids She closes silently.

"Oh!" cries the thinker, who, sickened and his heart swollen, sees her doing her work, "Accursed, accursed you are, destroyer of beings, detestable and cruel Death; may you be deluged and desolated by the ever renascent flood of immortal Life!"

The gravedigger has straightened up. She turns round; now she is made of pink and charming flesh; her amicable forehead is crowned with rosy corollas. She is carrying beautiful naked children in her arms who are laughing at the sky, and she says mildly to the thinker, while looking at him with eyes full of joy:

"I am, in fact, the Laborer who accomplishes relentlessly and endlessly the transformation of everything. Under my fingers, flowers turned to ash reflourish, and I am both the one you call Death and the one you call Life."

CX
ACADEMICS

"Ah!" says Madame Jeanne Thory, who is still charming in spite of the white threads sliding into her chestnut hair, to the Bishop of Golconda. "You've arrived just in time, Monseigneur, to know our thought, for we've decided to give our vote to Emmanuel de Just, In the final count, he's an amiable young man who knows his people like the back of his head, and has truly amused us this summer at Saint Enogat with the anecdotes he recounts so well, The die is cast; we're voting for him."

"Don't do anything of the sort, Madame," says Monseigneur Eucher. "I have, in fact, arrived just in time, but to enable you to avoid a grave error. Monsieur de Just has committed a bad action, the consequences of which will reverberate over his entire life, for one does not quit a woman, and he has notoriously quit Madame la Duchesse de Pouyet-Mallefer for that little scatterbrain Madame de Sines. Monsieur le Duc de Pouyet-Mallefer will never pardon that scandal, and he is right. Put yourself in his party; you will gain thus all his votes when he acts to have Monsieur de Glise nominated, to which it will be necessary to resign yourselves one day or other; but believe me, not right away!"

"Certainly," the Bishop of Golconda continues, lowering his voice, "you are, Madame, one of those whose beauty justifies a durable amity, but youth is cruelly ingrate. You would be prudent not to hasten the candidature of Monsieur de Glise, and not to permit him to give himself weapons, notably a talent that renders him sure of himself. So you ought to leave him at the *Revue* as long as possible. That way, at least you can be certain that he won't learn to write."

CXI
THE RING

At half past eight, as everyone is leaving the table, the chambermaid Juliette, tall, thin and correct in her tight dress, is at the top of the stairway hung with antique tapestries and ornamented with black marble negroes bearing flamboyant torches, when Monsieur le Marquis de Magnol, his eyes slightly lit up by Roederer and sherry brandy, goes past her on the way to his apartment.

"This evening," he says, "I want you—do you hear?—to come to my room for a moment, at about one o'clock, when I come back."

"From your mistress's room?" says Juliete.

"And why not?" says Marquis Joseph, philosophically. "You see, my child, these sluts in the grand style wear their embarrassment terribly, and on quitting them it's a true joy to find an amiable, natural girl with the scent of wild strawberries."

While speaking thus, the marquis, witty at times, goes into his room, after having slipped Juliette a little wallet in Russian leather, well-stuffed, which the soubrette promptly causes to disappear. Immediately, the coachman Félix emerges from some unknown hiding place in the shadows, red-faced, insolent and superb, coiffed in his Scottish cap; he gives the impression of being in search of a quarrel.

"Damn!" he murmurs, twisting his mouth. "It seems to me that Monsieur le Marquis disgusts you considerably."

"Monsieur Félix, when one has great ambitions, like you, and one wants to establish oneself as a carter in Decize, it's necessary not to pick fights, nor ask how the cook does her cooking. You'll doubtless be happy enough to have a good wife who can keep the house and receive the clients, and who doesn't mistake lanterns for electric light-bulbs."

"Wretch! A kiss, at least?"

"After the wedding," says Mademoiselle Juliette, chasing away her future husband, for at the same moment the student Lucien, the nephew of the Marquis, comes running.

"Ah!" he says to the tall soubrette, "if you only wanted to listen to me and hear me! But you don't know what passion and desire there is in my heart, and what treasures of amour!"

Then, maddened by the voluptuous curve designed by Juliette's dress, the boy raises a temeritous hand and inclines toward the imprisoned breast.

"Why," exclaims the ever-alert chambermaid, "that's a pretty ring!"

"Yes," says Lucien, looking at the ruby surrounded by diamonds, the ineluctable destiny of which nothing can any longer impede, "my Aunt Herminie gave it to me."

CVII
UTOPIA

The young Vicomte de Salar and Coralie Bredo reproduce accurately enough the celebrated painting in which Philippe II of Spain, in a court costume and a plumed hat, is contemplating his naked mistress, lying on a bed. Only, as mores have been purified since that time, Coralie is covered by a light transparent veil and the vicomte, tainted by impressionism and japonaiserie, is wearing an entirely violet town costume that, from the hat and the cravat to the silk stockings and the shoes, runs through all the symphonic scales of violet, singing its silent music with the most perfect dandyism.

Although very eccentric and singular, Antoine de Salar is visibly very innocent, and he adores Coralie with a sentimentalism borrowed from obsolete schools. He admires in silence the beautiful forms before his eyes, and suddenly, with a long sigh, says to his friend: "Dear heart, I would like to find a place to kiss, on your neck, your forehead or your divine arms, however small, that no one has touched or kissed before me."

The courtesan raises herself up, ruffled by such an audacious pretention. But after all, as she has been a student in the Latin Quarter, and as scientific problems do not displease her, she decides to admit the fabulous hypothesis, and responds tranquilly, with a philosophical mildness:

"In the final analysis," she says, "there might be one, and I couldn't swear to the negative, for everything exists in nature."

XXIII
REVENGE

Overwhelmed by the midday heat, the old Hellenist Mauriat is asleep under a beech, and his dear Pindar, stitched and striped with marginal handwritten notes, has fallen on his breast, open. Tanned, wrinkled and modeled by implacable study, the scholar is horrible and beautiful; his bushy eyebrows are like horsehair; his long nose is framed by profound creases, and his chin resembles a large apple. His stringy white cravat and his black suit, bruised and whipped by the clouds, no longer have human or inhuman form, but all of that is illuminated and transfigured by the flame of genius.

The Nymphs of the forest, who have perceived the aged thinker from afar, come running, their arms raised, their breasts exposed and their red hair unbound, and, numerous, urgent and smiling they lead their rhythmic dances around him, in order that he be charmed and believe that he has only seen them in a dream. But, mistaking for a large crimson flower the lips of the scholar, where so many divine songs have so often fluttered, a bee stings his mouth. Mauriat sees the Nymphs still leaning over him, who have just kissed his eyelids and his old parchmented forehead full of dreams.

But those dancers are not troubled for so little. They gaze at the scholar with amicable laughter, and, speaking for all her companions, Theano, her cheeks red with pleasure, says while making a fine curtsey:

"Excuse us, Monsieur and friend; we heard Greek!"

CXIV
THE LITTLE SCHOLAR

As it is Maman's birthday, and as there is a gala feast and a grand ball this evening at the home of his father the Minister. Little Lili has been given special permission to appear at dessert, to look at the garlands, the camellias, the sheaves of light and the heaps of flowers in the drawing-rooms and the boscage of the garden, illuminated by a magical gleam. But above all, the little girl admires her old friend Maas, who is disappearing under ribbons, crosses, stars, cordons and plaques. She has known him for a long time, forever; she is accustomed to digging her little fingers into the profound wrinkles that labor his face and playing with his soft white hair. But only today she has heard something that has intrigued her, and, leaping on to the old man's knees, she asks him whether it is true that he is a great scholar.

"Hum!" replies Maas. "In a certain measure. What about you? Are you a scholar too?"

"Certainly," says Lili, red and smiling.

"Well," says her friend, "do you know what there is in my pocket?"

"Of course," says Lili. "It's bonbons for me—fondants—and you've bought pink ones because I'm pink. Your turn now. Do you know what dolls think about?"

"No."

"Do you know in what books little birds learn their lessons?"

"No, my child."

"Do you know what the good God is made of?"

"Alas, no."

"Oh," murmurs little Lili, indignant and disconcerted. "Well, what do you know, then?"

CXV
THE ASSIZE COURT

The president has just pronounced sentence and the gendarmes come to take the accused away. The entire Ladureau family, father, mothers, sons, daughters and cousins of both sexes, has been condemned, some destined for the guillotine, others for the prison camp, exile or life imprisonment. However, the wretches do not seem desolate or terrified. Nothing has troubled their abominably decent attire, and they merely seem annoyed. Their ignoble faces express nothing except stupidity and the most vulgar platitude.

"Ah," says the old advocate Leil, whose wrinkled and intelligent face might belong to one of Daumier's advocates, to his colleague Remary, "look at those poisoners and loose women, more rascally than Messalina and Locusta; those cooks, as refined as Thyestes, those thieves, arsonists and forgers, that whole family more laden with horrors, crimes and incests that that of the Atrides! And observe that those creatures are not frightened, and how they resemble functionaries of a small town going about their duties."

"Indeed," says Remary. "That's because, like us, they possess free will, and, not having been besieged by hunger, by poverty or by devouring passions, they have not had to sustain any struggle, and they have embraced the career of murder as coldly as one enters into a bureau. They lack blood, remorse, bravery and the inevitable wrath of the gods. They're like ham actors devoid of talent and memory, who are playing a heroic tragedy in bourgeois costume—and without having put on their make-up."

CXVI
THE ENCHANTED ISLE

Intoxicated by the sight of marbles and shade, clad in satins and sitting with their lovers next to the bleak transparent river, the pale swains, overwhelmed by ecstasy, forget kisses and caresses and savor voluptuously the immense sadness of joy. In the distance, light murmurs are sometimes heard, of extinct songs, stifled sobs and vague clashes of arms; over there is life, struggle, the fatherland; but how can they, the lovers imprisoned in happiness, mingle with fêtes and battles, since between them and other men a high, sheer mountain looms up, which is lost in the azure? In the depths of their souls, however, they know full well that if they marched there bravely, the mountain would vanish and dissipate in the clouds. But they prefer to strive to believe that it is insurmountable, and they drown their thoughts and desires in yawning gulfs, in the vertiginous eyes of Cydalises, into which falls, somnolent and plaintive, an imperceptible stardust.

CXVII
THE AGED WOMAN

Oh, the aged, aged woman. who would believe that she is fifteen years old? Thus the terrible caricaturist Mattio sings in the middle of the ancient *Ronde séculaire* ballroom, in the midst of a group that has come to laugh and writhe, while listening to the story of Fonfride and Madame de Brielle. For there is no attenuating things! Lucien, as poor as Job and as handsome as an angel, has married in the depths of Poitou, for her money and no other motive, an aged, aged, very aged woman, who has not come to Paris for many years, and who is certainly as old as the streets and the monuments, for Parisians who are here present remember clear having seen, saluted and courted her at the première performance of *Les Burgraves* on 7 March 1843![1] It is known that the bizarre spouses have been invited to this ball, that they have accepted the invitation and that they will come—and as you can imagine, their arrival is awaited with a tremulous impatience.

They finally appear. O disappointment! O surprise! O triumph of the impossible and the supernatural! Is it wigs, garments, cosmetics and the genius of couturiers that have been able to realize such a fabulous miracle and transmute thus one of the Parcae into the nymph Salmacis? No, it is necessary not to seek to explain it by means of such simple and elementary reasons. Thin, frail, very small, one of those eighteenth-century

---

1 The reference is to Victor Hugo's historical play, the action of which takes place beside the Rhine in a hypothetical future.

waists that Richelieu held between his ten fingers, an infantile face, alert and knowing, with small, delicate and voluptuous features, cheeks more white and red than rosy, fiery little eyes, a riotous nose, arched lips, the ears of a Nereid. Hair—over a wig, what does it matter?—of the most seductive and playful blonde, such is the troubling marvel; and with his twenty-five years and his silky black beard, Fonfride is only just handsome enough not to appear ugly beside his adorable wife.

Quickly, in less than no time, all the rich, illustrious, celebrated noblemen with any sort of title have hastened around the little vicomtesse, and the women have gone pale, searching in vain for a fault in her irreproachable attire. Her neck surrounded at caressed by a necklace of primroses. Madame Céline de Fonfride is wearing a pale pink satin bodice embroidered with silver. Her shirt is short. Lilac with pink and silver flowers, with a broad ruche indented at the bottom, alternatively pink and lilac satin and silver cloth.

All the seams and all the edges of that princely robe are hidden and covered by garlands of primroses devoid of foliage. Her arms are entirely covered by long English gloves in pink leather, closed by diamond buttons. Finally, a charming eccentricity borrowed from a famous portrait of the time of Louis XIV, the slightly high bodice is perforated over the breast by three holes, with an enticing and irritating grace. Ancient jewelry formed by bright amethysts and pale pink corals mounted in silver, shoes in silver cloth and tender lilac stockings and a plume fan embroidered with primroses, complete the adornment of the ideally inebriating woman, who has, in an instant, rendered Paris mad with amour.

The other women? There no longer are any! The men all adore her, and she holds all of them, with a gesture, a half-smile, a wink or a word that she drops, charmed, educed, enchained, captive. Then, after Fauré and Mademoiselle Krauss,[1]

---

1 The composer Gabriel Fauré (1845-1924) and Gabrielle Krauss (1842-

she goes to the piano and sings, with verve, accuracy, measure and incomparable wit, an old song—but everyone affirms that her song is perfect, and resembles a necklace of luminous pearls unraveling in the night; she has not been able to force her young golden voice to imitate old age. People dance, and the pretty Céline is the queen of the dancers, lively, full of grace, as light as the breeze and floating dust, or a feather in the wind; and there are no more talkers, speech-makers or witty Parisians; no one any longer wants to see or hear anything but the little vicomtesse. She stands up to everyone and everything—men, women, delicate dishes, foaming champagne, the glare of the lights; she is the joy, the intoxication, the folly and the glory of the fête.

But while she is lifting her glass to respond to a toast that has been proposed in her honor, it seems that her body suddenly shrinks and diminishes; her face pales and fades, her eyes are extinguished; she falls, stiff and inanimate. Thus the ball finishes, by virtue of that catastrophe, the ballroom quickly deserted in the midst of a frightful and sinister tumult.

"In sum," says Mattio, going down the stairs, "what is it? A sudden congestion? The rupture of an aneurism?"

"No, Monsieur," the brazen voice of the celebrated Doctor Cloquemin, that rude octogenarian made like an oak, responds to him. "Madame Céline de Fonfride, who has just expired before our eyes, has died of *old age!*"

1906), principal soprano at the Paris Opéra.

CXVIII
THE WANDERING JEW

Under the rain, through storms, the fury of the skies in delirium, without pause, without rest, incessantly, the Jew is perpetually carried away through fields and forests, châteaux and cities, capitals and deserted plains, no longer on foot, as of old, but at the gallop of black horses harnessed to his berline. He is no longer clad in a red blouse and a leather apron, one no longer sees whirling around his head, on the breath of the tempest, long frightened tresses, as he was once encountered by the burgers of Brussels in Brabant. Today Baron Isaac de Laquedem has gone completely bald, like a polished rock, and his gray beard, a little long at the chin but very short over the cheeks, is trimmed in the latest fashion.

Although he ought not to stop in any ballroom, since he does not stop anywhere, Baron Isaac is, beneath his elegant overcoat trimmed with fur, in full official dress, with gloves and a white cravat, and his weighty shirt and black coat disappear under the ribbons, decorations, sashes, necklaces, crosses, plaques and stars of all the orders in the world. The bewildered crowd watches him pass by like a god, and a few imbeciles are even crushed under the wheels of his carriage. Women send him their best smiles, and blow him pretty kisses from the tips of their rosy fingers, and to all of them, without preference, the baron throws checks. A check, a check, a check, exactly similar to the one before, and always for fifty millions; for the man who once only had five sous now only has fifty millions, but he always has them.

When he passes before their palaces, very rapidly, the kings, hoping that he might get down, have red carpets laid out, the Queen of Sheba even calls out to him, and, brilliant in her garment of precious stones, says to him from her window: "Do you want to come up, pretty fellow? I'll be very amiable!" A waste of time; the horses always gallop furiously, and on the pavement burned by their hooves, sheaves of sparks spring forth.

Meanwhile, the Wandering Jew is dying of thirst, and often asks for a drink. If some gamin or farm-girl is sufficiently agile to hold out a glass of water or acidic wine to him at the right moment, he seizes it on the wing and slakes his thirst, and to Gothon as to the Queen of Sheba, as to dukes and princes, he throws his check for fifty millions in passing, having no other money on him.

And from one minute to the next, in his vertiginous course, he looks at his calendar chronometer, to see whether his thousand years will soon finish, and sometimes, too, he lights a very dry blond cigar and smokes it impatiently, while awaiting the Last Judgment.

CXIX
THE CHEERFUL VOYAGERS

Lying on his back at the foot of the mountain, the immense Monster opens his enormous fiery mouth, a gulf from which flames emerge, and he yawns hungrily, but without overmuch impatience, for he knows full well that he will be nourished and sated soon.

In fact, on the narrow road that snakes all the way to the summit of the green mountain, amid songs, cries and laughter to the sound of instruments, a dancing crowd advances, drunken, joyful and multicolored: soldiers on their horses, princes in long golden robes, scarlet-clad judges, artisans carrying their tools, mercers counting their bags of coins, young men and women coiffed with flowery hats, sensualists caressing young girls with bare cleavages, children picking flowers, rhymers making their lutes resonate, and august old men crowned with laurels.

Without slowing down their march, squires and cup-bearers serve them delectable dishes, which they savor, and pour them crimson wines to drink, and pages offer them the gold of their blond hair to wipe their hands. And laughing, chatting, singing, at an ever more joyful and hasty pace, they arrive at the top of the steep mountain, and from there, one by one, like thousands of stones hurled by an invisible hand, they fall into the gulf.

CXX
THE INEFFABLE

"What!" murmur the Souls, humiliated and looking at themselves with horror, "We, charged with sins and hatreds and soiled by funereal stones, are welcomed—O pity!—into the refreshing clarity of the True and into never-ending delight!

"O dear Souls," says the mild Child dressed in white in the clarity, calmly, raising his victorious finger, as when he spoke before the doctors, "don't you understand that forgiveness is an ever-overflowing river. Oh, don't shiver with fear, but on the contrary, launch yourself into a sure flight toward the candor of pure lilies and the immortal glory of roses! For the One who kneaded you with his hands can also wash away and efface your crimes in the flood of his immense love!"

And while the walls of iron, the sad lakes of ice, the citadels of bronze, the red fuming braziers and the terrifying circles of the Night fade away and vanish, azure themselves, the arches stairways and pilasters of paradise are piled up one atop another in the azure, in the distance, always looming up toward the palaces and gardens of joy, open, quivering, delighted, filled with the diamante light of innumerable infinities, and under the white glare of myriads of stars, the Souls, like a whirling flock of blue butterflies, rise up, charmed by the rhythm of the triumphant ode, all the way to the blazing whiteness where the vague reflection is already commencing of that which cannot be expressed with human words.

EPILOGUE

Mesdames et Messieurs, this is to have the honor of thanking you, If you are content, tell your friends and acquaintances. I shall now salute you and disappear with regard to showing you the magic lantern, but I shall not take long to re-enter by another door under the figure of a jeweler, a manufacturer and merchant of Cameos, for in these difficult times when skylarks so rarely fall from the skies ready roasted, it is necessary, in order to live on one's intelligence alone, to accumulate many industries and petty métiers. I am who speaking to you, in the old age at which I have now arrived, have worked hard, toiled and bent my back, and when shall I be able to repose?

Not, I think, on this needy planet, but after my final death, the One who deigns to have pity on avian virtuosos and the tiniest ephemeral insects will certainly be able, if he wishes, to give me a good employment. And who knows whether he might not permit me to return to my original estate as a rhymer? Perhaps I could render a few services, compose and rhyme very precisely the odes that are sung by the petty Angels in the inferior Heavens. As for the Cherubim, clad in light and surrounded by their great giant wings, I know full well that Orpheus and Pindar, Hugo and Gautier are not too many for them—but to each according to his merit.

Oh, certainly, in the gardens of delight where diamond lilies flower, I would certainly like to see the One who, awakening his great lyre, forces submissive lions and tigers to weep with love, and also the good Ronsard, clad in crimson, as he always longed to be, throwing roses into his flavorsome wine. I would like to see all the great Frenchmen: Rabelais first of all, Villon, who, enjoying eternal bliss, no longer fears being hanged; Clément Marot, delivered from the vile mask that our adored Master has put over his face, and La Fontaine, who has not had to learn wisdom by climbing the blue stairways of the Heavens, since he already had it. And above all, I would like to see Heinrich Heine and Aristophanes in their white garments, marching arm in arm like two brothers on the bank of a Eurotas with silver waves bordered by oleanders, admiring the heroic splendor of Helen with the beautiful hair, and the venerable head, as smooth as ivory, of the soldier Aeschylus.

If, however, because of the wicked deeds and faults of prosody that I have been able to commit, the good Lord God does not deem me worthy of entering into the True paradises, perhaps he will permit me to inhabit the enchanted isle of Watteau, where, with my comrades the petty poets—Glatigny,[1] among others—we can spend the time of eternity cheerfully.

Under the foliage, in the shadow of marble fountains, in the grass where Églé and Mademoiselle Aminte are sitting, in split satin dresses, holding oblong musical scores on their knees, we shall hear concerts of voices and symphonies of flutes and guitars. In my opinion, we shall also encounter in some green clearing Arlequin, Mezzelin, Scaramouche, white Pierrot with shoes tied with pink ribbons, and the other actors, not forgetting the pensive donkey with human eyes, who, to cheer us up with their gracious infantile games, excite before us so many pantomime dances.

---

1 Albert Glatigny (1839-1873) was greatly influenced by Banville's *Odes funambulesques,* and became his principal literary disciple, but died before he could fulfil his promise.

ADDENDA

DUET

As solidly as the citadel of Pergame on the high hill, a cylindrical bonnet is erected on the head of the pharmacist Hochedieu, around which run dementedly a garland of flowers embroidered in silk of various colors; and, like the waves of tumultuous seas when the sun drowns there in setting, bloody crimsons pursue one another, mingle and flee on his top-quality French cashmere dressing-gown, and become entangled in reckless arabesques.

The pharmacist's pretty wife Colette, with the white teeth and the little turned-up nose, is pouting, because it is Sunday, streaming with joy and light, and her husband will not permit her to go for a walk. And, as in the comedies of Molière, the husband and the wife are both talking at the same time, he in a loud voice and with noble gestures, she very quietly, and mentally. And it is thus that they exhale their souls, in these two speeches of exactly equal length:

"Colette," says the pharmacist, "never forget that I have raised you as far as me, and that you were born in a family of simple agriculturalists. Certainly, I don't begrudge you my benefits, which would scarcely be worthy of a great soul; but you ought never to forget them, and ought to recognize them by means of a tender and affectionate respect and the thousand delicate attentions that love invents and suggests. Undoubtedly, you cannot comprehend my subtle thoughts and the lofty combinations with which my wit plays, but idolatry is willingly unintelligent and it is pleasant to admire blindly.

Intoxicate yourself with the happiness, therefore, that consists of possessing, in the intimacy of every instant, a superior man!"

Thus speaks the pharmacist Hochedieu, while making his left calf tremble like Talma.[1] Meanwhile, the mute discourse of the pensive wife accompanies his with a musical exactitude.

"There on the Mail," Colette says to herself, "two paces away from us, handsome soldiers in red trousers are strolling, very becoming in their dolmans, who are gazing at women with eyes full of amour, and whose sharp moustaches are lifting their tips skywards, and who are charming, while my husband is abominable to behold. Oh, I might decide one day to listen to the advice of my friends, Madame Grif the notary's wife, Madame Danguis the bailiff's wife and Madame Célos, the merchant of novelties, and then, pharmacist that you are, there will be more officers in your life than there are on the market square on days of grand reviews, when the sun illuminates the scabbards of the sabers and makes the fringes of the epaulettes catch fire like a golden brazier!"

---

1 The actor François-Josept Talma (1763-1836), famous for expressing wild and intense passion.

PIERROT THE GOOD SON

In the pantomime, certainly less illustrious but perhaps just as instructive as the tragedy of *King Lear*, an old peasant has two sons, one good and one bad, and it is Pierrot who is the good son.

While his brother persists in persecuting the old man and making his life miserable, he, the stainless white Pierrot serves him, pampers his and caresses him, being, in his soul as well as his face, lily-white. When the father trembles with cold and shivers, he goes to fetch the blanket from his own bed and wraps him in it. But the bad son snatches that blanket away and puts it under his own feet, like a carpet.

Seeking another and more efficacious fashion to warm the poor old man, Pierrot brings him a bowl of hot soup, which the famished father devours gluttonously. The bad son thinks that he is eating too much, gives numerous signs of disapproval, and finally takes possession of the bowl; and, as the father pursues it with his avid lips, he applies to the back of his head a blow so powerful that his nose collides with the table and its tip is broken off.

Then, gripped by pity, with all kinds of tender precaution, the good son Pierrot seizes the tip of his father's nose with his agile fingers and piously, with a little saliva, sticks it back on.

A PARTIAL LIST OF SNUGGLY BOOKS

ETHEL ARCHER *The Hieroglyph*
ETHEL ARCHER *Phantasy and Other Poems*
ETHEL ARCHER *The Whirlpool*
G. ALBERT AURIER *Elsewhere and Other Stories*
CHARLES BARBARA *My Lunatic Asylum*
CHARLES BARBARA *Stirring Stories*
JULES-AMÉDÉE BARBEY D'AUREVILLY *Hannibal's Ring*
NATALIE CLIFFORD BARNEY *The One Who is Legion*
S. HENRY BERTHOUD *Misanthropic Tales*
MAY ARMAND BLANC *The Last Rendezvous*
LÉON BLOY *The Tarantulas' Parlor and Other Unkind Tales*
PETRUS BOREL *The Treasure of the Arcueil Cavern*
ÉLÉMIR BOURGES *The Twilight of the Gods*
ADA BUISSON *The Baron's Coffin*
CYRIEL BUYSSE *The Aunts*
KAREL ČAPEK *Krakatit*
BERNARDO COUTO CASTILLO *Asphodels*
JAMES CHAMPAGNE *Harlem Smoke*
FÉLICIEN CHAMPSAUR
   The Emerald Princess and Other Decadent Fantasies
FÉLICIEN CHAMPSAUR *The Latin Orgy*
ARMAND CHARPENTIER *Claustrophobic Madness*
BRENDAN CONNELL *Unofficial History of Pi Wei*
BRENDAN CONNELL (editor) *The Zaffre Book of Occult Fiction*
BRENDAN CONNELL (editor)
   The Zinzolin Book of Occult Fiction
RAFAELA CONTRERAS *The Turquoise Ring and Other Stories*
DANIEL CORRICK (editor)
   Ghosts and Robbers: An Anthology of German Gothic Fiction
ADOLFO COUVE *When I Think of My Missing Head*
RENÉ CREVEL *Are You All Crazy?*
QUENTIN S. CRISP *Aiaigasa*
QUENTIN S. CRISP *Graves*
LUCIE DELARUE-MARDRUS *Amanit*
LUCIE DELARUE-MARDRUS *The Last Siren and Other Stories*
LADY DILKE *The Outcast Spirit and Other Stories*
CATHERINE DOUSTEYSSIER-KHOZE
   The Beauty of the Death Cap
ÉDOUARD DUJARDIN *Hauntings*
BERIT ELLINGSEN *Now We Can See the Moon*
ERCKMANN-CHATRIAN *A Malediction*
ALPHONSE ESQUIROS *The Enchanted Castle*
ZDRAVKA EVTIMOVA *Laura and Other Stories*
ENRIQUE GÓMEZ CARRILLO *Sentimental Stories*
DELPHI FABRICE *Flowers of Ether*
DELPHI FABRICE *The Red Sorcerer*
DELPHI FABRICE *The Red Spider*
BENJAMIN GASTINEAU *The Reign of Satan*
GUSTAVE GEFFROY *Decadent Tapestries*
EDMOND AND JULES DE GONCOURT *Manette Salomon*
REMY DE GOURMONT *From a Faraway Land*
REMY DE GOURMONT *Morose Vignettes*
GUIDO GOZZANO *Alcina and Other Stories*
LUIGI GUALDO *Narcisa and Other Stories*

GUSTAVE GUICHES *The Modesty of Sodom*
ALTHEA GYLES *A Woman Without a Soul and Other Writings*
EDWARD HERON-ALLEN *The Complete Shorter Fiction*
EDWARD HERON-ALLEN *Three Ghost-Written Novels*
RHYS HUGHES *Cloud Farming in Wales*
J.-K. HUYSMANS *The Crowds of Lourdes*
J.-K. HUYSMANS *Knapsacks*
COLIN INSOLE *Valerie and Other Stories*
JUSTIN ISIS *Pleasant Tales II*
JULES JANIN *The Dead Donkey and the Guillotined Woman*
LIONEL JOHNSON *The Complete Winchester Letters*
VICTOR JOLY *The Unknown Collaborator and Other Legendary Tales*
GUSTAVE KAHN *The Mad King*
KLABUND *Spook*
MARIE KRYSINSKA *The Path of Amour*
BERNARD LAZARE *The Gate of Ivory*
BERNARD LAZARE *The Mirror of Legends*
BERNARD LAZARE *The Torch-Bearers*
JULES LERMINA *Human Life*
MAURICE LEVEL *The Shadow*
JEAN LORRAIN *Errant Vice*
JEAN LORRAIN *Fards and Poisons*
JEAN LORRAIN *Masks in the Tapestry*
JEAN LORRAIN *Monsieur de Bougrelon and Other Stories*
JEAN LORRAIN *Nightmares of an Ether Drinker*
JEAN LORRAIN *Princesses of Darkness and Other Exotica*
JEAN LORRAIN *The Soul Drinker and Other Decadent Fantasies*
JEAN LORRAIN *The Turkish Lady and Other Writings*
GEORGES DE LYS *An Idyll in Sodom*
GEORGES DE LYS *Penthesilea*
ARTHUR MACHEN *N*
ARTHUR MACHEN *Ornaments in Jade*
PAUL MARGUERITTE *Pantomimes and Other Surreal Tales*
HENRI MARTIN *Isuren*
CAMILLE MAUCLAIR *The Frail Soul and Other Stories*
CATULLE MENDÈS *Bluebirds*
CATULLE MENDÈS *For Reading in the Bath*
CATULLE MENDÈS *Mephistophela*
OSCAR MÉTÉNIER *Three Decadent Stories*
ÉPHRAÏM MIKHAËL *Halyartes and Other Poems in Prose*
LUIS DE MIRANDA *Paridaiza*
OCTAVE MIRBEAU *The 628-E8*
OCTAVE MIRBEAU *The Death of Balzac*
GAURAV MONGA *Costumes of the Living*
RICHARD O'MONROY *The Last Waltz and Other Stories*
CHARLES MORICE *Babels, Balloons and Innocent Eyes*
MANUEL MAGALLANES MOURE *What is Love*
MONTESQUIEU *The Temple of Gnide*
GABRIEL MOUREY *Monada*
DAMIAN MURPHY *The Acephalic Imperial*
KRISTINE ONG MUSLIM *Butterfly Dream*
OSSIT *Ilse*
PHILOTHÉE O'NEDDY *The Enchanted Ring*
CHARLES NODIER *Jean Sbogar and Other Stories*
CHARLES NODIER *The Memoirs of Maxime Odin*
CHARLES NODIER *Outlaws and Sorrows*

HERSH DOVID NOMBERG *A Cheerful Soul and Other Stories*
HERSH DOVID NOMBERG *Happiness and Other Fiction*
EDITH OLIVIER *Horror! Horror! Horror!*
GEORGES DE PEYREBRUNE *A Decadent Woman*
HÉLÈNE PICARD *Sabbat*
URSULA PFLUG *Down From*
JEAN PRINTEMPS *Whimsical Tales*
RACHILDE *The Demon of the Absurd*
RACHILDE *The Blood-Guzzler and Other Stories*
RACHILDE *The Princess of Darkness*
JEREMY REED *Surrender to a Stranger*
JEREMY REED *When a Girl Loves a Girl*
ADOLPHE RETTÉ *Misty Thule*
JEAN RICHEPIN *The Bull-Man and the Grasshopper*
FREDERICK ROLFE (**Baron Corvo**) *Amico di Sandro*
FREDERICK ROLFE (**Baron Corvo**)
     An Ossuary of the North Lagoon and Other Stories
ARNAUD RYKNER *The Last Train*
WILLIAM SEABROOK
     Astounding Secrets of the Devil Worshippers' Mystic Love Cult
ROBERT SCHEFFER *Prince Narcissus and Other Stories*
ROBERT SCHEFFER *The Green Fly and Other Stories*
MARCEL SCHWOB *The Assassins and Other Stories*
MARCEL SCHWOB *Double Heart*
COLBY SMITH *The Ironic Skeletons*
SIMEON SOLOMON *Collected Writings*
CHRISTIAN HEINRICH SPIESS *The Dwarf of Westerbourg*
BRIAN STABLEFORD (**editor**) *The Snuggly Satanicon*
BRIAN STABLEFORD *Spirits of the Vasty Deep*
COUNT ERIC STENBOCK *Love, Sleep and Dreams*
COUNT ERIC STENBOCK *The Shadow of Death*
COUNT ERIC STENBOCK *Studies of Death*
MONTAGUE SUMMERS *The Bride of Christ and Other Fictions*
MONTAGUE SUMMERS *Six Ghost Stories*
ALICE TÉLOT *The Inn of Tears*
GILBERT-AUGUSTIN THIERRY *Reincarnation and Redemption*
GILBERT-AUGUSTIN THIERRY *Stigma and The Pompeiian Fresco*
DOUGLAS THOMPSON *The Fallen West*
FELIX TIMMERMANS *A Peasant Farmer's Psalm*
TOADHOUSE *What Makes the Wave Break?*
LÉO TRÉZENIK *The Confession of a Madman*
LÉO TRÉZENIK *Decadent Prose Pieces*
ANNA JANE VARDILL *The Secrets of Cabalism*
RUGGERO VASARI *Raun*
ROGER VAN DE VELDE *Crackling Skulls*
ILARIE VORONCA *The Confession of a False Soul*
ILARIE VORONCA *The Key to Reality*
JANE DE LA VAUDÈRE *The Demi-Sexes and The Androgynes*
JANE DE LA VAUDÈRE *The Double Star and Other Occult Fantasies*
AUGUSTE VILLIERS DE L'ISLE-ADAM *Isis*
RENÉE VIVIEN *Lilith's Legacy*
RENÉE VIVIEN *A Woman Appeared to Me*
ILARIE VORONCA *The Confession of a False Soul*
ILARIE VORONCA *The Key to Reality*
TERESA WILMS MONTT *In the Stillness of Marble*
KAREL VAN DE WOESTIJNE *The Dying Peasant*

www.ingramcontent.com/pod-product-compliance
Lightning Source LLC
Chambersburg PA
CBHW020412110726
47899CB00006B/1956